"Rose Little, I'm mad at you."

Rose blinked up at the giant man who had just interrupted her with a kiss.

"Excuse me?"

James didn't retract his words.

"I'm mad at you, Rose Little. I'm mad that you left without saying anything and I'm mad that you didn't answer my call. I deserve some kind of check-in to know you're okay after everything you've been through. That we've been through. I know you're Wildcard Rose, but sometimes I think you use that as a pass to run headlong into danger and it's okay."

Rose started to say something—she wasn't sure what—when he continued.

"And that's what I thought I was mad about before you got here. You, being you, running into the unknown swinging. But then I saw you and I realized I'm really just mad at me. I'm mad that I didn't give you a good reason for you to take me with you. So I'm going to make sure I give it now."

AGAINST THE CLOCK

TYLER ANNE SNELL

INTRIGUE

This book is for Doc Ernest and her retirement. My favorite background character who has popped up in almost every story I've written is finally passing the torch to her daughter. For readers who caught on, just know she's on a private beach somewhere with a very handsome man at her side and an extremely yummy drink in her hand.

Recycling programs for this product may not exist in your area.

ISBN-13: 978-1-335-69052-4

Against the Clock

For questions and comments about the quality of this book, please contact us at CustomerService@Harlequin.com.

Harlequin Enterprises ULC
22 Adelaide St. West, 41st Floor
Toronto, Ontario M5H 4E3, Canada
www.Harlequin.com

HarperCollins Publishers
Macken House, 39/40 Mayor Street Upper,
Dublin 1, D01 C9W8, Ireland
www.HarperCollins.com

Printed in Lithuania

Tyler Anne Snell lives in South Alabama with her same-named husband, their artist kiddo, four mini "lions" and a burning desire to meet Kurt Russell. Her superpowers include binge-watching TV and herding cats. When she isn't writing thrilling mysteries and romance, she's reading everything she can get her hands on. How she gets through each day starts and ends with a big cup of coffee. Visit her at www.tylerannesnell.com.

Books by Tyler Anne Snell

Harlequin Intrigue

Manhunt
Toxin Alert
Dangerous Recall

Small Town Last Stand

Search for the Truth
The Deputy's Secret Double
Against the Clock

The Saving Kelby Creek Series

Uncovering Small Town Secrets
Searching for Evidence
Surviving the Truth
Accidental Amnesia
Cold Case Captive
Retracing the Investigation

Visit the Author Profile page at Harlequin.com.

CAST OF CHARACTERS

Rose Little—After a daring rescue leads her to a new wave of fame, the wildcard deputy of Seven Roads is targeted in a series of deadly attacks. To survive them and stop her attacker, she must team up with the only man who refuses to let her run into danger alone.

James Keller—The only mechanic in town has led a careful life in Seven Roads since his adoption as a child. But when he is saved by a fiery deputy who leaps before she looks, he'll throw caution to the wind if it means helping keep her safe.

Liam Weaver—The McCoy County sheriff, he does everything in his power to help keep the past from hurting one of his own.

The Bus Passengers—The people who Rose helped save, their rescue earned her the title of hero.

The Reporter—A mysterious man who might be following Rose, he seems dead set on writing her story no matter its ending.

Derrick Tillman—The one person Rose couldn't save, his death started a deadly chain reaction that could end them all.

Chapter One

Rose Little didn't want to talk about it. No way, no how. She wanted to stay tight-lipped, closemouthed, quiet as a mouse.

The man, wearing a nice button-up shirt with a skinny tie and holding a business card he was trying to Houdini into her hand, was begging that she do the opposite.

"We don't mind paying for the story," he said, not for the first time since he had met her outside the coffee shop. "We just want an exclusive so it can reach more people. Don't you want to share your good deed with the world?"

Rose didn't know which annoyed her more: the reporter trying to cash in on her two minutes of fame or the fact that he'd chosen to do so on her off day. Normally she would be wearing her deputy's uniform and her McCoy County Sheriff's Department badge but right now she had on a good pair of jeans and an old sweatshirt that was multicolored, faded and always comfortable despite outside annoyances.

Off days were rare for a department so small. They were even more rare for the smallest of that small.

Rose loved her work.

She just wasn't a fan of bragging about it.

"Doing a good deed is enough for me," she said, stepping around him on the sidewalk. Her car was in the lot behind the business complex. It seemed that the reporter didn't mind the extra few yards to it. He got into line next to her, unfazed.

"Oh, of course, of course," he said. "I'm not trying to say you did it for the fame or anything, I'm just saying that this is truly inspiring and a really good comment on courage in the face of danger. It's not about you getting recognition, it's about creating hope for others."

Rose was the first person to admit that her last name was unfortunately a very accurate description of her physically. Rose Little was petite. Only an inch over five feet, she could put on a Halloween costume and go trick-or-treating as a child without anyone suspecting she was actually a thirty-two-year-old woman.

Most times it didn't bother her—she had spent years becoming mighty despite her size—but walking alongside the reporter, she found their height difference to be annoying. She wanted to frighten him away with what her colleagues at the sheriff's department called her scary eyes.

Green little daggers that let whoever was on the receiving end of them know that they had managed to get on the diminishing side of her patience.

But Rose couldn't do that to this man. Not only did he keep his attention ahead of them, he was a full foot or so above her. She would have to grab him by the collar and pull down to really level him out.

And she had a feeling Sheriff Weaver wouldn't be a fan of that.

So, she settled for a verbal attack. Passive but pointed.

"I don't see how what I did would inspire hope for others. Not many people find themselves trapped in that kind of situation every day."

The man rounded the street corner with her.

He was shaking his head.

"The point isn't the people, it's you," he said. "Not many people would have risked their lives like that. You were a hero, saving the day by yourself and doing it like you were in an action movie. I mean, you've seen the video, right? It went viral for a reason. The entire country is talking about—"

Rose could see her car in the distance. She didn't want to see the man anymore.

"Listen—" she stopped to face him "—I get that this is your job and that there's a lot of people who might eat a story like me up even though it's been months, but I don't want to make this a big deal. Because it wasn't, really. I didn't do it for fame or fortune or comments. I did it because it needed to be done. So it was nice to stroll with you, but this is where that ends."

Rose wasn't entirely heartless. She'd been born and raised in Seven Roads, Georgia, and had spent a majority of her life in most of the same spots since. She knew there was a Southern etiquette, and she tried to practice some with the reporter to help the rejection go down easier. So she held out her hand for a shake, thinking that was it.

The man took her hand, only to push forward his own agenda.

She felt the business card against her palm before she could stop him.

He smiled big, taking the rejection with stride.

"I'm sure you'll change your mind," he said. "And when you do, call me at this number."

Rose watched as the man retreated as fast as he had popped up. It left her a little dumbfounded. She had expected a lot more buzzing. She slipped his card into her pocket—she wasn't going to litter—and went to her car, glad for one less annoyance for the day.

That lack of annoyance didn't last long.

Her car started lurching and the check engine light went on before she could make it back to the house. Rose was glad it had at least waited to act up when the reporter wasn't around. He would have no doubt eaten it up had he seen her car—*the* car from her "daredevil rescue"—was having issues.

"There's no way I'm letting anyone get wind of this," she told herself aloud. She patted the dashboard. "Don't worry. We'll get you fixed, keep avoiding reporters, and eventually everything will die back down. They'll find another story more exciting than me, and we can keep on living our lives without the world caring."

The car didn't talk back but it did shudder here and there as she changed direction toward the only mechanic in town.

Rose didn't blame it one bit.

She should have taken it to the shop after everything had happened.

However, life had become…a lot after what she had done. Not just from reporters. The town of Seven Roads held gossip longer than grudges. Five months later, she still was stopped on occasion at the grocery store to chat about it.

Sure, Rose could admit what she had done was a little more than what some might have. And yeah, she had potentially saved several people by putting her own life on the line.

But…she hadn't been able to save everyone.

It was a fact that so many seemed to gloss over from the word jump.

Rose's hand tightened around the steering wheel.

She knew the truth, no matter how indifferent the rest of the world seemed to be about it.

A world hadn't ended with a bang but a whimper.

And she seemed to be the only one who had remembered the sound.

Now all she could do was hope for the quiet again.

JAMES KELLER WAS having a pretty decent day so far.

The old Maxima he had been having trouble with was done, fixed, paid for and gone. The same went for the engine issues with an even older Buick and Mrs. Jones's usual oil change and tire rotation. James had even dealt with Mr. Donahue's impromptu drop-in for a stay-and-chat session.

He had updated James on the neighborhood's latest news, given his opinion on his grandkids' current obsessions, and gone as far as to bring up his recently divorced daughter Layla again.

"Now that she's dropped that baggage of that sorry husband of hers, I'm ready for her to get a nice, good guy who knows value when he sees it." Mr. Donahue had given a pointed look over to James at this. "Someone who runs their own business because he's a good son and an even harder worker."

James had nodded along with the sentiment but hadn't taken the bait. While he did indeed run Keller Auto, the only mechanic shop in Seven Roads, to help his father, he didn't want that, his work ethic, or Mr. Donahue to be why he reentered the dating pool. He had exited it for good reason two years beforehand and wasn't sure dating or marriage was in the cards in his immediate future. Something he had told the older man a few times before. But, as with a lot of folks in Seven Roads, James's thoughts on the subject didn't seem to matter much.

So, getting Mr. Donahue to leave the shop without much fuss had been a feat. One that, along with his shrinking to-do list, had contributed to his good mood.

A good mood that was still holding in place when an unscheduled job drove up into the dirt lot that surrounded Keller Auto.

A good mood that stayed mostly strong when he realized who was behind the wheel.

A good mood that only slightly wavered when the driver got out with an expression that looked ready to turn everyone else to stone.

Deputy Rose Little, the wild card of Seven Roads, walked up to James in the garage bay with absolute purpose. Her small frame was an odd contrast to the set of her brow and gaze. James wasn't a longtime local, but he had been told quickly that Rose wasn't someone you could judge by appearances.

And that was before what had happened outside of the hospital's research annex a few months ago.

James reined in the urge to think Rose looked particularly cute today, with her dark hair done up messy and wearing a fluffy, colorful sweater, and instead put down his notebook to greet her.

Or, rather, listen to the greeting she threw his way.

"I would have called but my car started struggling a few minutes ago. The engine light came on too. I thought it would be easier to just drive it here while I still could." She thumbed over her shoulder back at her car. "Do you have time to look at it?"

As far as James knew, Rose didn't exactly know him. He'd never had a chance or need to talk to the deputy before. But that didn't mean he didn't know of her tendency to rush in first, ask questions later. The hospital annex situation was the most sensational story yet.

Not that it was just some story. One of the people she had saved had recorded the whole event and posted it online. Then it had gone viral.

Some worshipped her, some praised her simply. A spare few blamed her. Some said she had done too much in an attempt to get some attention.

James knew *of* Rose—not who she really was—but he doubted her heroics had been for glory.

Rose Little had rescued a busload of people from a terrifying death, all while narrowly avoiding the exact same fate. James had watched the video too—who hadn't in Seven Roads?—and didn't need to have been there in person to understand just how close she had come to losing her life.

If she had done that for fame and glory only?

Well, then she probably would have greeted him with her name first, her problem second. As it was, she was standing there looking expectantly at him with a small scowl across her face.

James wiped his hands on his coveralls from habit and nodded.

"As it happens, I'm having a light day, so I can take a look now." He gestured toward the open bay behind him. "Drive it in and I can get started."

Rose gave one curt nod and did as she was told.

James watched, noting the car drove okay, but there was a sound he couldn't place as it moved. He was running through the possibilities when Rose appeared at his side. She explained what had happened and did a brief rundown of the car's history.

It was an older model but had been mostly rebuilt by her over the years.

Which told James that what she had done during her rescue hadn't just been luck.

She was good with cars.

"My dad was in a wheelchair a lot when I was a kid, so I became the one in charge in our family for everything car-related since middle school," she said, as if hearing his thoughts. "Whatever is tripping this thing up, it wasn't because of an error on my part at home. There shouldn't be any problems on the maintenance side."

James eyed the tires.

She must not have missed the move. She sighed.

"The tires have recently been replaced," was all she said.

If she was expecting him to ask about the research annex, she didn't show it. James respected that. He didn't bring up anything to do with her job and instead focused on his.

"You can wait in the main building while I take a

look if you want," he offered, grabbing a light. When she didn't budge, he added, "Or you can hover here."

He worried it sounded snarky the second he said it, but Rose didn't take it the wrong way. She nodded and stayed put.

If she had been an attention seeker, he thought that would extend to him. Talking his ear off, regaling him with her own glory. As it was, he forgot she was there at all until a few minutes later into his check.

"Do you have a maintenance record?" he asked. "Or did you do most of it yourself?"

At this, her resting scowl woke up.

"I did the maintenance I could myself but kept records for both my own work and when I had to get a new transmission put in out of town once. The records for both are in the glove compartment. I also have a running log I keep at home if that doesn't work for you."

James raised his hands in defense.

"I'm sure what you have is fine." He had been at the hood but now moved around to the passenger's-side door. He opened it and leaned over for the glove box.

This was a move he had done countless times in his career.

Lean over, reach for the glove compartment handle, open and take out what he needed. All while never even touching the seat.

But, for whatever reason, James did something slightly different this time.

He sat down on the seat before reaching out.

That was where he messed up.

That was where their problems began.

Because no sooner had he lowered his weight onto

the fabric than three things happened almost at the exact same time.

There was a *click* sound.

Followed almost immediately by the feeling of something shifting below him.

Then, as his brain and body both processed what he was hearing and feeling, the third thing happened a breath later.

Rose Little grabbed his wrist and, despite her small size, she said something in a voice so commanding and quick that James couldn't help but listen with every fiber of his being.

"Don't move a muscle."

Chapter Two

The space between a good decision and a bad one was, according to Rose's late grandmother, only as long as the finger that wags.

"People sure aren't as self-aware as they should be," she'd told a younger Rose once. "Most don't know they're doing wrong until someone is yelling it at them. You know, wagging that finger in their faces. Especially us Little women. We're so dang confident in ourselves that we need a good person to tut at us from time to time. To show us we might have made a choice we shouldn't have. Or, we're barreling toward one we should avoid."

Grandma Little had then lovingly looked at her husband, sleeping next to her hospital bed, and smiled.

"Just make sure the finger wagging at you belongs to someone worth listening to or else it's just some silly nilly wasting your time judging you."

Rose was staring at James Keller's coveralls, smelling car oil and sweat off him and the garage around them, and knew she didn't have the time to wonder whether or not he was someone worth letting judge her choices.

Mainly because of the bomb strapped beneath the man's hide.

"I'm going to have to ask you to elaborate on that *don't move* command," James said through a terse line of his mouth. To his credit, he moved very little while delivering the request.

Rose was careful not to move too much herself, worried that he might subconsciously mimic her, but there was no easy way to answer.

So she didn't mince her words.

"I think there might be an explosive under the seat. One you just triggered by sitting down. That was the click I heard and, I'm guessing you felt something beneath you too?"

He didn't nod but he did confirm.

"I felt something like a click."

Rose looked down.

There was no easy way for her to look under the seat, even with the door open. Not without the man moving for her. Even while sitting, James was undeniably a big man. Tall, tall and taller with legs that matched his stature inch for inch. His knees almost touched the dash and, had he not sat down at an angle, there wouldn't be any space between at all. Despite Rose being the very opposite in size, she couldn't see a way for her to get around them to look beneath the seat. At least, not without moving him.

And *if* she was right, that could spell a big ol' *boom* for both of them.

"A bomb," James said flatly. "You're saying I'm sitting on a bomb."

Rose tore her eyes up from his legs and the floorboard. He kept his gaze forward, his head not moving at all.

"I can't get a good look from here," she said. "I'm going to try and look under the back of the seat. Hold on."

Rose wasn't going to let a second slip by without some kind of action tied to it, so she did as she said and opened the back door behind him as gently as possible. James's voice carried easily to her despite his lack of movement while speaking.

"I know you're law enforcement and all, but how familiar are you with explosives? Is that even in your list of skills?"

Rose wasn't about to fault the man for doubting her abilities. Mainly because he wasn't exactly wrong to be skeptical. She stepped back, kneeled outside of the car and then angled her hands and head into the empty floorboard with more care than she had ever put into peeking at anything before.

She didn't respond until after the top of her head was lifted off the floor mat once her peeking was done.

She went back to standing next to the stationary mechanic a few seconds later, hand hovering near her back pocket where her phone was currently residing.

"I've just done some cursory training but, no, I'm nowhere near an expert in explosives. But I think we should probably stop talking and not move until I call in some backup to see what they say."

"Is there something really there? A bomb under the seat?"

Again, it wasn't like Rose could fault the man for asking.

She pulled her phone out and brought up the sheriff's number directly beneath her finger.

If the mechanic had been someone else, someone showing a lot more fear than he was, Rose would have put on her gentler verbal gloves. But there was something sturdy-feeling about this James Keller. Rose trusted in his sense of self-preservation.

So she stayed blunt.

"I'm about ninety percent certain it's an explosive with a pressure plate. One you triggered, and are keeping from going off by sitting on it. Shift your weight too much and it'll detonate. But I can't see enough of it to be absolutely sure about any of that. So I'm going to call in the right people who do have the skills to figure it all out."

The line of his jaw got mighty tight at that. For a second Rose worried he would nod. Instead, James Keller gave her a terse one-word.

"Understood."

Her finger hovered over the call button but her mind was sticking to the why of it all. If there was an explosive beneath the seat, why? Who did it? Why the passenger's side and not the driver's?

The call started, the ringing loud enough that it echoed slightly in the garage around them. It would have carried more had the bay they were in not had a door wide open to the outside. No sooner did she have the thought they were lucky to be alone in the shop than dirt kicked up in the distance at the road. A beige truck was driving into the lot. The windows were tinted enough that she couldn't see who was inside.

"Someone's pulling up," Rose said, already taking a

step back. "I'm going to tell them to leave and be right back. Is that okay?"

Rose's priorities had stacked in an easy order the second she heard the click beneath James.

Keep the civilian safe.

Remove James and the bomb without anything and anyone taking damage.

Two simply stated goals.

Now they shifted to make room for another.

Keep civilians from getting into danger.

Then the other two priorities on repeat.

If James had his own list, he showed that they at least synced up on this want. James Keller was nothing if not impressive. He gave her another one-word answer.

"Go."

Rose hurried out of the bay while the call continued to ring. Her mind went on dual trains of thought as she decided to call the sheriff's department directly next, while also thinking of what she should say to get the mechanic shop's customers out of danger without causing a town-wide panic.

She had never been a nifty talker like other people in her department—Deputy Collins could talk someone into oblivion yet seemingly manage to never annoy said person—but Rose believed tact might be needed here. If only a little. Dealing with this situation, whatever it may be, would be a lot easier if all of Seven Roads didn't drive up after the news undoubtedly spread like wildfire.

The truck stopped a few yards off, almost where she had stopped to talk to James when first arriving, when another vehicle drove up behind them and into the lot.

It was a lot smoother than the first, older truck with its dents and rust. This one was an upkept black 4Runner with dark tint that matched the first.

Rose slowed her gait. The call went to voicemail in her hand. She didn't hang up. The 4Runner stopped next to the old truck.

Sheriff Weaver's voice was low as his to-the-point, prerecorded message asked the person calling to leave their details. He promised to call them back after.

Rose watched as neither driver exited their vehicles.

If the thing beneath the passenger's seat wasn't a bomb, that would be a great—and embarrassing—misunderstanding. She would hear about it for days, weeks, probably the occasional comment through the years. The sheriff wouldn't say much—he was a quiet guy, like their only detective, Darius, was—but Price and the few other deputies in the department? They would use the incident in good humor as long as the situation had an opening for it, like older brothers teasing a sister.

It would be annoying for Rose.

However, if she wasn't wrong? If someone had planted an explosive in her car—*the* car—then that changed everything.

It gave her a bad guy with bad intentions.

A bad guy who probably wouldn't just lurk in the shadows if their handiwork found its way to a mechanic's shop, of all places.

A bad guy who might bring backup.

Still, Rose stopped walking and gave the two vehicles a look of reproach.

Maybe they were simply friends or from the same

family, coming to the mechanic's shop for oil changes or tire rotations at the same time. Maybe they weren't getting out yet because they were on their phones or not even paying attention to the woman standing a few yards away, phone in hand and staring.

Maybe—

The beep of the sheriff's voicemail stopped her from going down the question rabbit hole.

Instead she let her gut talk.

"I'm at Keller Auto and I think we're about to have a big problem."

The truck's driver's-side door swung open.

It was a good thing she was already running.

The gun that aimed her way sure didn't give her much time to do anything else.

THE DAY HAD taken a turn. There were no ifs, ands or buts about that. James had gone from a quick workday and right into an unbelievable nightmare.

Was he really sitting on a bomb?

Who even did that anymore?

At least in some place as tiny and mild as Seven Roads, Georgia?

But you're in Wildcard's car, he reminded himself no sooner than he'd questioned the why of it all.

Wildcard Rose wasn't some tiny little name in a tiny little town anymore. At least, she hadn't been in the past several months. She was the deputy who had made national news with a viral video of rescue that had been movie-worthy.

Not all attention would be wholly good, right?

But that also didn't mean her getting targeted with

an explosive beneath her car seat was the next, logical step. Her passenger seat to boot.

Maybe it wasn't a bomb. Maybe it was a prank or something else that reminded her of the same kind of explosives that were in movies like *Speed* and *Lethal Weapon.*

Maybe we're just overreacting and this will be one heck of a story to tell Dad and Mr. Donahue later.

James mentally nodded his head to himself—he wasn't chancing movement just in case, regardless of how impossible it seemed to be sitting on a pressure plate was—and decided this would just be an inconvenience. One he would have to endure a little longer.

It was a weirdly calming thought.

One he held on to with great effort as a gunshot tore through the air behind him.

The sound was an explosion all its own and, having involuntarily reacted by jumping slightly, James thought for a moment that *he* had been the one who had exploded. His hands had moved up in front of his chest, like he was ready to fight the sound, but as far as he could tell, nothing else around his personal area had changed. Explosion or otherwise.

He registered the fact that it must be a gunshot a second after.

James wasn't a stranger to the sound, but he couldn't understand why he'd heard it here of all places.

It only made sense that Rose had been the one to fire the shot.

A breath later and the woman in question was at his side again. However, there was no gun in her hands.

"How do you shut the bay door?" she asked. Her

breath came out in a pant but there was power behind the words. It pulled an answer from James before a question.

"There's a chain on the left side next to it. Yank it and it'll fall."

She was gone before he finished.

"Don't move!" Her warning came only a few seconds before the familiar clank of the chain James had pulled slowly and with caution over the last several years sounded. He braced himself for what he assumed came next.

James couldn't see it, but he sure heard and felt the metal garage door slam into the concrete floor beneath it.

"Does it lock?" Rose yelled out to him.

Again, he answered without wasting a moment.

"A latch in the middle! The bar secures into the ground!"

James could only see the back wall of the shop. Pegboards with tools, a workstation that doubled as a counter that ran the length of the wall, and the only door and its one way to access the never-used traditional front of the shop. The door that led into the office was to his left, out of sight, and to his right was the only other engine bay with its track clear and pit matching the one Rose's car was sitting over now.

Which meant he had no idea what had gotten the woman more stressed out than the potential bomb beneath his seat.

It must have been enough to have her feel more comfortable locking herself in with a bomb.

After he heard a quick movement somewhere behind

the car, James finally had to do what any normal person might in this situation.

He finally asked some questions.

"What's going on? Did you just shoot at someone, or did they shoot at you?"

He could hear Rose talking but realized it wasn't at him. The urge to turn in his seat was so intense his muscles tightened to resist. He was about to ask again when the small woman managed to fill the entire space next to him in the doorway.

She was empty-handed still.

But she wasn't panting anymore.

In fact, Rose Little looked frustratingly calm.

Which made what she said next even more wild.

"I have some good news and some bad news."

Chapter Three

Rose was sweating. Her heart was racing and there was a hitch at her side. There was also blood on her right hand, something she only noted after trying to wipe some of the sweat off her palms in preparation for what happened next.

Blood, sweat and tears—not that she was crying—didn't do much up against bombs. Or guns. Or men who appeared at a time that was too coincidental to not connect to the former, seemingly with no problem using the latter.

Yet in all the quick chaos, there was one thing that surprised her the most.

James Keller hadn't moved.

At least, not enough to count.

Rose hoped their luck stayed true through this next part.

"The good news is, we don't have to wait a while for the experts to show up before we move you," Rose continued from her earlier statement, not giving the man room for a response. This time, though, she did pause a little as she looked at the space between the open car door and the concrete pit of the bay next to them.

James used the pause well. He got right to the point.

"What's the bad news?"

Five feet, give or take, Rose decided of the distance. She moved to the spot she thought was directly between the two points of interest and bent her knees slightly. Then she went through an imagined motion of pulling something from one side to the other.

It might work.

"The bad news is we don't have to wait for the experts to show up before we move you," she answered.

James said something but Rose's attention split again. At the far side of the room the door she had blocked shook violently. The men had realized she had locked the bay doors. Now they were trying to come in through the office.

Rose kept her voice as still as the surface of a lake but even she could tell there were definitely about to be ripples in it.

"How deep is the pit beneath this car?" she asked.

"The service pit? This one is around five feet five inches with the wooden floor in."

"And the one next to us?"

James was quick.

"Six feet. There's no floor in it."

The opening didn't seem as wide and there were metal tracks for the vehicles in the way of those four feet. The closest track to them might be a problem.

But it wasn't like they had many other options.

The door across from the garage started to take more damage. The men were ramming it with something.

Rose realized it was time to get very specific with her new mechanic friend.

"I don't have my gun and there's at least two men

with their own trying to come in. They're going to make it in before backup gets here. I can't defend you and I can't leave you, so I'm going to move you instead."

Rose was actually thankful that James couldn't turn to look directly at her. She guessed his expression wouldn't be kind. Instead, he parroted her intentions with notable grievance.

"You're going to move me?" he asked. "Doesn't that mean that if I'm on a bomb, that bomb goes off? No offense, I'd rather you leave me than blow me up."

Rose got close to him, no need to bend over too much given her short height.

"We're not going to blow you up. We're going *to hope* that there's a small delay between you leaving the seat and the explosive going off."

"So what if there is? We'll still get the blast right after."

He couldn't see it, but Rose thumbed over her shoulder.

"Not if we jump into the service pit. The concrete should—" Rose was cut off by a noise she had been hoping not to hear.

A gunshot.

In this context, an impatient one.

It looked like their mystery combatants were getting frustrated. Though she had no idea why.

Either way, Rose had to wrap this up.

Now.

"We're going to jump into the service pit behind me and hope that covers us," she said.

James's jaw was a hard line. She could see sweat had already formed along his neck. The effort of not moving was a lot more taxing than most people might think. A bead of sweat rolled down the side of his face as he said *no*.

"You leave," he added. "If there's a delay then I can make it to the pit myself. You run out the back now."

His words were surprisingly resolute.

Rose was more so.

"You're too tall and you've been cramped in there for too long, so you're probably going to lose time just trying to stand and get out," she said. "You need momentum as soon as possible. So I'm going to give it to you."

Rose wrapped both of her hands around James's arm that was closest to her. It wasn't enough to trigger the weight shift, but it was enough to get James to slightly turn his head finally.

His eyes were a mix of green and brown. There seemed to be some gold in there too, blurring the line between.

It was nice.

"You don't need to do this." His voice was deep and low but sounded louder than the men trying to break down the door.

"But I am," she said. "Now, I'm going to count to three and on the word *Go* we're going to throw ourselves as fast as we can into that pit."

James was silent for the briefest of moments.

"What if there's no delay and this thing blows sky-high the second I'm off it?" he finally asked.

Rose knew it wasn't a smiling occasion, but she couldn't help it.

"If that happens, then I promise you, we won't know it."

The gravity of her words probably didn't have time

to sink in. Or, maybe they did. Whatever weight they held for James, he seemed to make a decision after that.

It timed almost too well with the toolbox and chair that had been propped against the office door finally clattering to the ground.

They were now at the true now or never.

Those hazel eyes with their gold in-between hardened.

"On *Go*," he said.

Rose nodded.

Then she counted down from three.

James's adoption had been a quiet one. He had been seven and in foster care for three of those seven years. He'd known his biological parents, but in the last little while had grown to think of them more as simply people he visited once a month in a small room at the department of human services. If anything, it was his social worker, Ms. Bell, that he had grown a deep attachment to over the course of their time together.

So when her sister had offered to take him in when adoption was finally put on the table for him, James had felt some excitement. He would still get to see Ms. Bell all the time.

It was a silver lining that he clung to through his parents' rights being terminated, through his visits stopping, through the rocky year of waiting for the courts to catch up to him, and even when he told the judge he was ready to be the legal son of the Keller family.

They were good, nice people and he would have a good, safe home.

But then Ms. Bell went and moved out of state for her husband's job.

It was only as they watched the moving truck pull away that the then-seven-year-old James thought he finally understood what a sinking feeling in one's gut really felt like.

A part of him felt like he had given up his biological mother for the maternal love of Ms. Bell, only to realize that, at the end of the day, she had been doing her job.

Now the job was done, and Ms. Bell had moved on in both the literal and physical sense.

At nine years old, James's new sinking feeling came from the intense and sudden worry that he had made a wrong choice somewhere along the line. That, even though he knew he hadn't actually had many options, he had still somehow misstepped.

And now everything had changed and there was no going back for a redo.

That feeling had grown and stretched as James had grown and stretched as he got older. It was still there sometimes, a lurking worry, but not as it first had been. Then, as he had reached the age of thirty, he realized it had become more of an ache. An echo. He could get to *it* but it didn't often get to *him*.

However, for the first time since he was a child, James felt that sinking feeling come back to life, strong and loud.

That helpless fear that he'd made the wrong choice and now the world was forever changed for it.

The pain registered first but he couldn't place exactly where it was on his body. It all hurt. He hurt everywhere.

He wasn't lying down but he wasn't on his feet either. He also wasn't sitting. He was, instead, lopsided.

James blinked a few times. An almost overwhelming sense of nausea turned in his stomach. That was when he realized what he had been hearing since opening his eyes.

Ringing. In his ears.

And that was it. No other sounds.

Just pain and ringing.

What had—

All at once the car, the bomb and then the gunshots pounded through his memory. Then the confusing world around him started to make sense.

He had made it to the bottom of the second service pit. Despite the distance, despite the bomb's blast, despite the men banging their way through the garage to them. Unbelievably, James had made it.

His gaze was pitched up and there he saw one of the metal tracks they used to service the vehicles overhead. It was still above but warped and bent, not completely intact anymore. That might have had something to do with the giant-something partially lying across it.

It was part of a roof—the Keller Auto roof—and past that he could see a strip of sky.

It was a startling contrast. One that finally pushed James even closer to reality.

The rest of the details finally sharpened.

There *had* actually been an explosive beneath the car seat, and it *had* gone off. Debris was all around the pit and the smell of smoke and burning things was so heavy it clogged his nostrils. There was no telling how badly the rest of the garage was damaged but the pit itself had actually held. At least, it had kept its structure. The debris still falling was an issue. James caught a burning something next to him on the ground. It was paper, small, but actively on fire. On reflex he palmed it out.

The movement hurt, but not because of the flame.

There was a weight on his side, and it had taken until now to notice it.

That sinking feeling nagged again.

The most important detail inside the service pit had come last.

Rose Little did in fact seem little. She was a deadweight lying against him, her back to his side, head pressed against his rib cage. Her hair was splayed out across her face and only the downward turn of her lips could be seen through it. James couldn't remember how they went from the car to six feet down, but Rose had obviously taken a bigger blow than he had.

"Deputy Little?" Her name came out warbled and wrong against the ringing in his ears. James used the hand that had palmed out the small paper fire a second ago, unable to worry about the soot it had left behind, and gently held her face against him.

Rose wasn't moving.

James shifted his weight slowly, holding her, until they were both sitting up.

He called her name again, but the woman remained slack against him.

He couldn't tell if she was breathing—there was too much going on around him—so he moved his fingers to her neck.

Then he held his breath.

What felt like a lifetime stretched between nothingness and then a beat.

Her pulse.

James wanted more confirmation. He sidestepped any modesty and placed his large hand spread out against her chest.

He held his breath again.

Then felt hers go out.

If James wasn't currently forming a human cage around the woman, he would have let relief wring him out. Instead, he gave the deputy's body a cursory look.

There were no protruding bones or obvious and alarming injuries as far as he could tell. Her clothes had seen better days, and she was somehow missing a shoe, but there wasn't anything that spelled immediate issues.

Well, other than the fact that she was out cold.

And they were in a pit in the ground of a burning building.

Then there was the whole *men with guns* business.

Had they been in the blast or far enough away like them that they had survived?

James was seized by a coughing fit. He kept Rose tight against him until it passed.

She had said backup was on the way but he couldn't just sit and wait for them.

James winced into that pain he couldn't exactly pinpoint and slowly pulled them both to their feet. Rose definitely wasn't faking her condition. She was a rag doll in his arms as he stood to his full height. He stepped on debris and over clutter, holding Rose against him like a groom ready to walk his bride through their bedroom door.

Flames and heat and smoke and pain danced around them.

Holding her was easy. Getting out might be a different story.

James took one quick look down at the slack face resting against his chest.

Wildcard Rose Little looked relaxed, peaceful even.

"I can't defend you and I can't leave you."

James nodded and spoke his resolve, even though he and the woman he was holding couldn't hear his words.

"Don't worry. I'm not about to leave you either."

Chapter Four

Rose didn't wake up until the next day. To be more exact, she didn't wake up until early the next morning. So early that the darkness outside of the hospital window threw her for a moment.

Not as much as the overwhelming pain that went through her head the moment her brain seemed to connect the dots around her.

Beeping machines. Something in her arm. A bed. Not her clothes.

Hospital.

She wasn't dead.

She was in the hospital.

Rose didn't have the time to take comfort in that fact before nausea bowled her over. She might have realized where she was but that didn't mean she was fully oriented. She jolted up, covered her mouth and looked over the side toward the window, hoping that there was a trash can to catch what was about to happen.

There wasn't.

There was, however, a takeout bag.

It appeared like magic right where it needed to be just as the pain in her head came from her mouth.

There wasn't time to feel self-conscious about it either. She couldn't spare the time to worry about the hand that touched her back as it happened or the low rumble of the voice behind the action.

"I did the same thing," he said. "Just don't be like me and refuse the pain meds when they offer them the first time."

The hand was heavy and warm and stroked a small path there on her back until the waves of nausea finally stopped. Then the warmth was gone, along with the bag. A tissue found its way to her next.

Rose wiped at her mouth and let a shaky breath out.

A doctor she hadn't seen before took the bag she'd just gotten sick in and headed out to the hallway without another word. He was back a few moments later.

Rose took the remote attached to her bed and pressed a button to adjust the bed until she was sitting upright. She leaned back and sighed as the man mimicked the lean on the couch next to her. He met her eye when both had settled, and smiled.

"Now that you're awake, I have some good news and some bad news."

James Keller looked like he was the bad news. His hair was tousled, maybe wet, his face was bruised, and there was a split in his eyebrow. It was a crack above a stare that felt kind and patient and unbothered. There wasn't an IV attached to him and he wasn't wearing a hospital gown like Rose, but she could see he was wearing loose sweats and a baggy T-shirt. He was probably bandaged somewhere. She thought there might have been a wrap of some kind on his wrist. But she also wasn't on her A game and the lighting wasn't the best. There was a lamp on in the corner and backlights around the machines, but the overhead light was off.

The clock read 3:00 a.m.

She noted James was wearing slippers, not full shoes. Was he a patient still?

He arched an eyebrow at her obvious inspection.

She fought to focus back on what he said.

"Good news and bad news, huh?" she repeated.

He nodded.

"Are we a good news first kind of lady or a Band-Aid rip off kind of gal?"

Rose didn't have to think on that long at all.

"Rip it off."

James clasped his fingers together. He rested his hands on his lap, a picture of relaxation. Which made his words quite the contrast.

"The bad news is, you were right about the bomb," he started. "I don't know the details—I'm assuming you'll find out more and faster than me—but from what I've been told it was attached beneath the passenger's seat, and I really did trigger it by sitting on it. The sheriff came in here all hot about it and said he has some experts doing their job to figure everything out and that they'd update me when they had an update. But, again, I'm sure you'll get more than I will, considering you're the law. And, well, it was also your car."

Rose had already figured that she had been right about the bomb. If only for the fact that she'd woken up in the hospital in pain. And the next morning. The blast or the fall must have knocked her out. The last thing she remembered was pulling James.

After that, not a thing.

"The good news?" She had a lot more to ask and say but that seemed to be the better to aim at.

James undid his hands to point a finger gun at her.

"The good news is, you were right about the bomb."

It was Rose's turn to arch her eyebrow in question.

James explained with a smile.

"Most people would have thought they were jumping to conclusions and not some character in an action movie. But you jumped and landed right on the truth." His smile fell. He sobered a little. "Your sheriff said that if you hadn't acted as fast as you did, there were a few separate times we both probably would have bitten the dust. So, good news that you were right, and you acted when you did. And thank you for that."

Rose heard the sincerity.

She had heard the same before.

It made her…uncomfortable.

She smiled to be polite and gave a little nod.

That nod took her smile and rattled her pain back to the forefront.

James's eyebrows knitted together.

"I saw the nurse in the hallway earlier. She said the doc will be here in a minute but let me see if I can't hurry him—"

Rose waved her hand to cut him off.

"I'm okay," she said, pushing through a wave of nausea and hoping her statement was true. "I'm concussed, right?"

James didn't look convinced, but he did nod.

"You have some bruising too. Oh, and two stitches on your leg. I didn't see it but the nurse had me look away while she checked so I think it's probably high up there."

He paused while Rose did a quick inspection.

Sure enough, there was a bandage on her upper thigh and hip. Right where her underwear should have been.

Good on the nurse for having James turn away.

Though it did pose a question Rose hadn't thought to ask about yet.

"You've been here since earlier? Why?"

A look Rose couldn't place passed over James's expression and tugged the corner of his lips down. He seemed to think carefully before he answered but it was simple enough.

"They said no one else was coming."

An uncomfortable heat climbed up Rose's neck and started to slide onto her cheeks. It wasn't embarrassment—she wasn't embarrassed at her lack of emergency contact—but it wasn't all gratitude either. Instead, she had traveled back five months prior to the same hospital but on a much different floor.

She was staring at a doctor, seeing her lips move as she spoke, but all Rose could focus on was the body covered by a sheet behind her.

Derrick Tillman hadn't had an emergency contact either.

And because of Rose, he would never need one again.

"Hey, don't go getting all weird about it." James's words broke through the memory with surprising ease. Rose let her gaze refocus on the man. He waved a hand as if wiping it away. "I have a thing about hospitals," he continued. "When I was a kid, I woke up in one alone and it really did a number on me. Now I try to make sure that it doesn't happen to others if I can."

He dropped his hand and snorted. There he was, playing nonchalant again. Casual and cool.

So very far from what Rose was currently feeling.

"But you did save my life," he pointed out. "The least I could do was keep you company to say thanks."

It was true, she supposed. He was there because he was thankful. Because he felt indebted.

Rose didn't like either feeling.

She tried to smile into the new discomfort and play it off.

"Well, thanks, but next time don't worry about me," she said. "I don't mind waking up alone. If something was really wrong, though, I'm sure the sheriff would pop in to check up on me. It's just a hazard of the job."

James rolled his eyes. Actually rolled them like some annoyed teenager. Yet, the look was oddly intriguing on him. Like a massive man being called Tiny. He was at odds with his own image. Rose couldn't help but give him a questioning look in return.

"I've never been in this situation before, but I think you're really underselling the whole saving us from a bomb thing," he said. "Most people would probably have already filled this room up with flowers and cards and would be trying to name their kids after you. I think waiting for you to wake up to say thanks is way less than you should get."

Rose felt that heat again, moving up her neck.

Again, it wasn't embarrassment, but she couldn't quite figure out the feeling.

Instead, she tried to match the man's casual attitude with her own.

"I don't do what I do for praise." She sighed. It hurt.

She certainly was going to be sore for several days. "If I wanted flowers, I'd buy them myself. If I wanted a kid named after me, I'd have my own and name them myself too. Helping people is the job. I shouldn't be doing it in hope of getting something in return."

After the bus incident she had seen the room full of flowers, heard the cries of gratitude, and undying promises to return the favor. Rose understood wanting to thank someone who had helped them, but to do so much and stretch that gratitude out… Well, it made her skin crawl.

Did that mean she wanted James to leave now?

She wasn't sure.

His eyes seemed to find something in her expression that was interesting enough. His gaze didn't leave her as he opened his mouth to say something, but the door opening to her left stopped him.

It was the doctor—someone Rose was more than familiar with. He had a nurse with him, and he looked caught between a man doing his job and a father about to scold a child for doing something reckless.

This was what she was used to, this was what she wanted.

No special treatment, just treatment.

Rose didn't speak to James again after that. Not in as much detail as before at least. Somewhere between the doctor summarizing her injuries and talking about what happened next, James left.

After the doctor and nurse had gone, Rose looked at the spot where he had been sitting. She closed her eyes after a while.

The next time she opened them, sun was peeking

through the slit in the blinds over the window. Someone was taking up the same space, but it wasn't him.

Deputy Price Collins had his phone in one hand and a coffee in the other. He grinned when he saw that she was awake.

"Even on her off days, Deputy Little manages to set the world on fire," he said in greeting. "When I say you could have your own TV series, I'm not at all exaggerating."

Rose didn't mean to, but in the moment, all she could think about was the man who had sat there before, smiling at her.

Then, she wondered where James Keller was.

Then she wondered why she had wondered that at all.

THE MAIN MECHANIC at Keller Auto might have survived the explosion but the shop itself hadn't been as lucky.

James fiddled with the bandage on his forearm before dropping his hand deep into his coverall pocket. There was no reason to wear what he normally worked in, since the building in front of him could no longer be considered a building. Or, at least, a safe one.

The explosion had been small, he was told. Minor compared to what most thought of when the word *bomb* came into play. That was the only reason why he and Rose had survived at all. It had been a targeted attack, meant to decimate the vehicle it was hidden in.

And the people sitting inside.

"On top of that, I'm not sure the person who made it knew their stuff. I'm told it was *sloppy*," the sheriff had said at their last conversation earlier that day.

Sloppy had almost been enough.

For the building, it surely had been.

Keller Auto had stretched across the middle of a two-acre lot and was just over 4,000 square feet, shop, lobby and office included. Most of that space had been the two bays themselves.

Now the building had been halved. The first bay had exploded, and the second bay had gone down in the aftermath. The lobby and office hadn't suffered from the impact but the small fires that had broken out had eaten through most of the former. The fire department's hoses had brought on the final damage, water destroying the bulk of what the fire hadn't.

Only a few items had survived the impact, the aftermath and the rescue.

Those were in a plastic tub sitting in the back of Mr. Donahue's RAV4.

He was wholly apologetic. Every part of his face seemed to fall all over again as he patted the top of the container.

"One of my nephews was on the fire crew," he started, motioning with his other hand to the fallen Keller Auto. "He knew how important this place was to your and your daddy's history, so he thought quick and managed to grab a few things. Sorry it isn't more."

It had been three days and two nights since the bomb had gone off. It felt like nothing and a whole lot of everything all at once. James didn't think he was overwhelmed yet. Maybe, instead, he was still circling shocked.

He didn't feel much at all when he gave thanks to the older man.

"The fact that anything was salvaged is a good

thing," he said. "I'll have to thank your nephew in person some time. And thanks for coming out to give it to me. I can't say when we'll have a place for you to come around for a chat again, though. Dad's been dealing with the insurance people, but we can't do much until the investigation is over."

Mr. Donahue was all solemn.

"It's tiring enough to be a walking miracle. You don't need to add apologizing to it too."

They stood for a moment, not saying much. James had been surprised that Mr. Donahue hadn't joined the masses trying to get gossip out of him since leaving the hospital. It had been a jarring experience. Mostly because all the people who had come asking after him had actually just been trying to get information on the woman at his side.

Wildcard Rose had made the news again.

And everyone wanted a piece of her.

Even now, it irritated James.

"What happens next, then?" Mr. Donahue asked, forgoing the questions he probably really wanted to ask. James was grateful for his restraint.

"Dad's still at my uncle's, so I told him to just stay there, and I can handle anything that pops up here." James shrugged. "As for everything else, I guess I'll take it a day at a time. There's not much else I can do."

Mr. Donahue nodded, but after James said it, he thought of the deputy.

There had been one question he had asked the sheriff, more than one time.

Keller Auto might have taken damage, but it was Rose Little who had been the target. And, if the bomb hadn't been proof of that, the men who had disappeared between the explosion and the sheriff's department showing up certainly had been.

James *did* want to know what happened next, but not for himself.

Chapter Five

Rose didn't know what to expect in life anymore, but she did guess that during her three-day stay in the hospital, a reporter or two might eventually find her. To the hospital's credit—and the sheriff's department's best attempts—no one made it past the invisible line outside of her room. At least not until the last day there.

Rose was sitting next to a vending machine, hand wrapped around a water and an empty candy wrapper on her lap, when a man sat down next to her wearing a smile. There was a cast on his arm and hand. She recognized him with a deep sigh.

"It sure is a small world, isn't it?"

The reporter from the parking lot the morning of the explosion gave her a smile and a small wave of the arm in a cast. He wasn't in a hospital gown but was instead sporting a collared shirt tucked into professional-style dark khakis. His hair was shaved close to the scalp and helped confuse her about where exactly his age fell within the thirties or forties bracket. He *looked* young but oddly felt older. The hospital's horrible fluorescents probably weren't helping that sentiment either. No one looked good beneath them, she had woefully decided after seeing her reflection in the bathroom mirror that morning.

Rose didn't feel the need to pull up a polite smile yet. It wasn't like they had met on the street again, after all.

"Living in McCoy County means always living in a small world," she said. "I could throw a rock in the lobby and probably hit one or two people I grew up with, whether we like that fact or not."

The man bit out some laughter. It didn't feel forced, but it somehow didn't feel genuine either.

Rose realized then that she had never actually learned the reporter's name. The business card he had slipped into her hand she'd placed into the pocket of her jeans. Those jeans had been stripped off and thrown away by hospital staff after the explosion.

Now, at her second meeting with this man, she had no name to anchor him.

It bothered her.

"That's true," he said. "Sometimes I forget that there are people who just stay forever in small places like Seven Roads. Just because I can't imagine wanting to, doesn't mean it isn't the plan others follow."

He was smiling. With or without his name, she found that she still wasn't a fan.

"And yet I've run into you twice in McCoy County in as many days," she pointed out. "If you're not a local then there must be something good that keeps bringing you back."

The man laughed again and Rose regretted not eating her last hospital snack in her room. At least she had already ditched her hospital gown. Thanks to Deputy Collins's wife, she was wearing an old high school T-shirt and a pair of dark sweats. It wasn't exactly her uniform, but it made her feel a lot more secure than the gown had.

Though that sense of security didn't do much as he turned to face her directly.

"And what if I said you were that good thing I'm sticking around for?" he asked.

Just as she wished she had on more professional clothes, Rose was internally berating herself for leaving her new phone back in her hospital bed. She didn't know where her conversation was about to go but she felt deeply that avoiding it would be her best play. Now she didn't have her phone to use to help her excuse herself.

So she reverted to the only other tool all Southerners wielded in the face of strangers.

Rose decided to be polite. She smiled. Before she could reply, though, he swooped back in.

"I was in an accident when I was leaving town," he explained. "I came back today to give thanks to the staff here and then saw you sitting here alone. I may not be here for you, but I can't just ignore *the* Rose Little either."

Rose was surprised at the sudden and aggressive urge to wish this man *would* ignore her. She didn't dislike reporters in general, but since her rescue at the research annex, she had become wary of them. And that had been before her adventure with the car bomb.

Rose glanced down at his hands to see they were empty. If he was wanting to record her—or already trying—whatever he was using wasn't out in the open.

"I'm not that interesting," she said, meeting his eye

again. "If you're looking for a good story, I promise it's not going to be with me."

"Says the deputy who's become quite popular lately for always acting like an action hero." His smile managed to stretch even more. At this rate it would fall off his face. She was losing the polite battle.

So Rose took a breath and decided to be blunt.

"Listen, I'm sorry you were in an accident too, but if you're chatting with me now hoping for an exclusive or something you can post about what happened a few months ago or a few days ago, you're going to be disappointed. Everything I've said before, right now, or in the future is off the record. And honestly, I'm not going to say anything remotely interesting enough for any record to begin with. What happened, happened."

She balled up her candy wrapper and stood with as much authority as she could muster while looking nowhere near professional.

"Now, I have things to do, so I'll be leaving," she continued. "I hope your recovery goes smoothly and you make it back home without any problems this time."

Since there was nothing more to say Rose assumed the conversation was over. She started to turn away, relieved that her hospital room was empty at the moment.

However, the man clearly wasn't done.

He stood to his full height, a great skyscraper to her ground-level height. Then he balled his hand at his side into a fist.

Rose went on high alert.

"You know, just because you act the hero doesn't mean everyone is ready to bow at your feet and treat you like one. I was just trying for conversation, I don't need to know who you ticked off to suddenly have them going to such extremes to teach you a lesson." His smile stayed and his fist relaxed into a hand against his thigh as he spoke. However, his words had lost their shine. "You've given yourself too much credit, Deputy Little. I don't actually care about you at all."

Rose's high alert has switched to an overwhelming need to defend herself. She didn't think she *was* that interesting. She wasn't trying to give herself any kind of credit either. Hadn't he been the one who had followed her less than a week ago, praising her? Asking for her story? Had she really misunderstood his intentions?

She didn't find an answer before the man's gaze went up above and over her shoulder in a quick flit.

That smile kept. His words were absolutely sharp.

"And on that note, I think it's time to go," he said. "I have my own schedule to keep."

He was quick to leave the hallway—Rose was slow to realize what had grabbed his attention before he left so abruptly.

She turned around, looking for whatever the man had seen.

Or who, rather.

James Keller was a wall of man, wrapped in coveralls. His arms were crossed over his chest, and he was watching after the reporter's retreating back without Rose even remotely blocking his view. There was a plastic shopping bag hanging from one of his wrists, but it did nothing to take away from the sheer amount of intimidation his stance was exuding. His deep voice was just as formidable as he addressed her without looking down.

"Who was that guy?"

Rose momentarily forgot herself. She blinked up at James with an eyebrow clear to her hairline.

"Wait. Why are you here?" she returned instead.

James shook the plastic shopping bag on his wrist.

"I heard you were still in here and thought you might want some food since the cafeteria is going through renovations. I didn't know what you liked, so I made some sandwiches. Who was that guy?"

He spoke in one, nonchalant breath until he got to the repeat question. He wasn't happy. It pulled Rose back to her senses. She turned to see the man, but he had already disappeared from view.

"He's a reporter," she said. "He tried to get an interview from me earlier this week about the—well, the other thing I went through. I turned him down. I thought he was going to ask me for another interview just now."

"What's his name?"

Rose's brow knitted together.

Once again, she hadn't learned the man's name.

If that was a note about her character or his, she didn't know.

She shrugged.

"If his business card had survived the explosion, I'd tell you."

James made a noise that sounded vaguely like disapproval. His expression convinced Rose even further of that theory.

"Don't talk to him anymore," he rumbled out.

Rose's cheeks heated at his words. She poked his chest through it.

"Hey, now. Why are you telling me—an independent, smart, and capable woman of the law, by the way—that I can't talk to someone?"

The poke did its job. His chin, and stare, tilted downward.

Green, brown and gold came together in a stare that fell the foot or so between them and right down into Rose's upturned gaze. It was only by the grace of God that she kept her expression frozen when he answered her, voice deep and brimming with certainty.

"Because I don't like him."

ROSE TOOK THE turkey and cheese sandwich. James took the peanut butter and jelly. They were eating both twenty minutes later when the doctor gave the all clear for Rose to leave. She made her sandwich disappear almost as fast as she went through the discharge process.

One minute they were eating, the next they were standing outside of the hospital.

Rose stretched her arms out wide and made a show of letting the sun hit her face.

Like James, there was some bruising across her skin. It was faded but there. Though Rose didn't seem like the kind of person to care much. She shouldered her bag and pulled out her phone with a heavy sigh of relief.

"I would very much like to *not* be back here anytime soon," she said. "I'm not knocking the service, but I'd rather not see this place for a long, long time."

James couldn't see what she was doing on her phone, but he guessed she was trying to arrange a ride. When Mr. Donahue had heard the news that she was still in the hospital, James had been sure that at least one person might be hovering around her. If only for protection's sake.

He'd thought it was more than appropriate to check. The food had been an afterthought. One he thought had been unnecessary as he'd walked off the elevator and saw Rose and a man chatting at the vending machines.

It had taken less than the walk between them to realize the man was not anyone she was friendly with. Never mind his balled fist or the smile that looked so forced.

However, Rose had been James's biggest red flag. He hadn't been able to see her face, but her body language was *off.* Considering James had seen her look more relaxed with a bomb strapped to the car they were sitting in and standing next to, her posture told him everything he needed to know.

Maybe he should have explained his bad vibes to the woman herself, instead of acting like some kind of jealous boyfriend. Instead, he'd simply given her a sandwich and been fine with not talking about the reporter again.

Now James couldn't help but wonder again if Rose actually had a boyfriend, jealous or otherwise.

"Is someone coming to pick you up?" he asked, deciding to get right to the point. "If not, I don't mind giving you a ride."

Rose shook her head, eyes still on her phone screen.

"I didn't know when I was going to be discharged, so nothing was set in stone for anyone to get me," she answered. "I'm just letting the sheriff know I'm out right now. I want to see him before he benches me completely from the investigation."

Her head turned with a swivel. Her eyebrow was raised.

"By the way, have you gotten any updates on the case? Has anyone asked you any more questions or anything?"

It was James's turn to shake his head.

"I was told I would be contacted if anyone needed anything else from me. I also got a promise that I'd be called when the investigation was over so I could follow up with the insurance company for the shop."

An expression he couldn't place flashed across Rose's features. She looked like she wanted to say one thing but decided against it in the moment.

"So you're probably not working today, then, are you?"

That conversational swerve threw James off, but he answered quickly with a no. It surprised him further when she nodded to herself and smiled.

"Then I'll take that ride," she said. "But I have one condition first."

James could have pointed out that giving her a ride was a favor, one that would help her out and not him, but the way she was staring up at him, almost excited, had his interest piqued.

He couldn't help it. He asked her what she meant.

"What one condition?"

Wildcard Rose didn't miss a beat.

"I need you to come home with me."

Chapter Six

There were a few things Rose realized that maybe she should have earlier in the day. The first was a pretty simple statement.

She was too comfortable with James. They weren't strangers anymore, but it wasn't like they were friends. Seven Roads might have been small, but it wasn't like they had been social beforehand. She knew of him, maybe even had shared a small nod or two in passing through the years, but that had been it. Even after the explosion, their status hadn't changed much.

James had been there when she had woken up in the hospital, sure, but after their talk he had gone about his way.

Then, days later, he'd given her a sandwich.

Now he was giving her a ride. To her apartment.

A place she rarely invited anyone over to visit.

Was it because of what the sheriff had told her the last time they had spoken in the hospital?

"From what I know of James, he probably won't boast about it…but I have to tell you that man went through a lot getting you out of the auto shop," Liam had told her. "Or at least what was left of it. I pulled up to the scene with Price, both of us ready to dive in until the fire department showed up, but instead we saw him carry you out of that nightmare like it was nothing."

Rose *hadn't* known that it had been James who got her out. He surely hadn't said as much during their talk. It made her feel an odd kind of guilt. She had tried to play it off.

"Well, I am pretty small," she had said. "Compared to him, especially. Carrying me should have been easy."

Liam hadn't let that sit a moment before he had humbled the comment.

"Easy or not, he cared a whole lot. I saw y'all when you came out—James was a cage around you. He wouldn't even give you up until the EMTs were pulling at him." Liam had sighed. It was anger but not at James. Still, he had some good words left for the man. "I also saw the inside of the shop. Getting you two out was a dangerous job in itself. He could have left you. He could have left you to get through the fire and the debris on your own. Instead, he managed to get you to safety and stay by your side, no questions asked."

No questions asked.

That observation was holding true.

Why wasn't James asking more questions? Could he still be in shock almost a week later? Was he waiting for privacy outside of the hospital instead? Or was he as nonchalant in his everyday life as he had been while sitting on that bomb?

Where did that calm and cool end?

And, was that the reason why Rose felt so comfortable around him in the first place?

It was like James Keller had become walking meditation.

Rose kept using her time with him to accidentally self-reflect.

It was unexpected. And annoying.

She was glad for the distraction of her cell phone ringing. It blared out the theme to *Jaws*. Rose saw her driver chuckle before she answered the only person that ringer was assigned to when they called.

"Sheriff," she said once the call connected.

Liam was quick and loud.

"Where are you? Price said you had discharged?"

Rose motioned to the truck around her though he couldn't see it.

"Yeah, the doc cleared me, so I left a few minutes ago," she answered. "I'm almost home. Why? What's up?"

Liam was somewhere noisy, but it seemed like a nice kind of noise. There were kids laughing and dishes clinking. Rose eyed the clock. It was lunch.

"I was hoping to grab you before you left. I want you to come to the department."

It wasn't a request.

"What's wrong?" she asked.

Despite the nice noise in the background, the sheriff's words were pure authority.

"Just get over here now."

THE MCCOY COUNTY Sheriff's department was small, like its staff. If someone wasn't paying attention they could almost pass it off as a large house nestled near the woods. An oddly shaped one, but a house all the same. Rose had once mentioned this comparison to Price when they were on patrol. He had laughed and told her that she only saw it as a house because her job was her whole life.

Wasn't it less depressing to think of the place you see the most as your home instead of a small building that once had Marty Fletcher mistake the jail cell cot as a toilet in the basement?

Rose knew she should have felt bad or worried about the comparison, but she just couldn't bring herself to agree.

She let out a sigh of relief as the building in question came into full view through the windshield. The world changed every day. There was comfort in the fact that the department rarely ever did.

"Are you sure it's okay for me to come in?"

James parked the truck in the guest spot out front. He wasn't as at ease as she was, that was for sure. In fact, he was showing more stress than he had when sitting on top of an explosive.

"It's not like I have a car to drive here myself," she pointed out. "Plus, you deserve answers as much as me on what happened at the shop. That's probably why I'm being called in anyways. It's more cost-effective to just come in together."

James nodded, absently.

"Sure, I guess."

Rose gave him a questioning look but didn't pry. Not everyone was comfortable around law enforcement. That wasn't a fault to poke at.

At least, that was what Rose thought until James glued himself to her side on the walk up to the front doors and blurted out exactly what he was thinking.

"I know I'm not here to get into trouble or anything,

but I have some childhood bad memories with the law and a cow can't change its spots." He put an arm around her shoulders and dropped his voice into a whisper. "Can we pretend you need my help to walk and that's why I'm here?"

Rose looked up at him with an expression she hoped showed nothing but being dumbfounded at that.

He saw the look and rolled his eyes.

"Not everyone has nerves of steel like you, Deputy Little. Let me feel needed so I can feel safe. Plus, I can't get in trouble here if I'm your plus-one. So let's have a nice cooperation." He started walking forward, his arm like a sling around her. Pulling her along with him was easy. Partly because of his height, but mostly because Rose allowed it.

Let me feel needed so I can feel safe.

James had said it so casually, in one breath, that someone else might have glossed over it entirely. Yet, Rose knew there were roots to the meaning of the phrase. Roots that went deep into the man's past.

Because Rose knew what James Keller had gone through as a child. Day two in the hospital and her curiosity about the man had seduced her to the dark side.

She had gossiped with Price, one of the few career locals she trusted to be as accurate as they were discreet.

That was how she'd found out about the time James woke up in the hospital alone.

She wasn't going to blame him now for being wary. Rose shrugged James's hand off her shoulder but kept in step with him.

"You can hold my elbow," she grumbled out. "But

the second we're in front of the sheriff you better be hands-off."

"Yes ma'am," he said, voice still low. His hand closed around its designated spot. He was gentle, even if his hand was calloused and rough.

Rose only hoped no one inside made a fuss over it. She *had* been blown up after all. A helping hand didn't seem too outrageous only a few days after.

There's that being too comfortable with James Keller thing again, she thought to herself, realizing how absurd it was of her to accept his request.

Yet, Rose didn't try to pull away either. Not even when James lowered his voice again and rumbled out another question.

"Can you limp a little or something? You know, really sell it?"

Sympathetic or not, comfortable or not, Rose narrowed her eyes at him.

"James Keller, don't push your luck."

JAMES KNEW ABOUT Sheriff Liam Weaver the way he knew about Rose—everyone in Seven Roads had done their due diligence when he had first moved to town. James had gotten most of his details from Mr. Donahue about the newcomer then.

Sheriff Liam Weaver was ex-military, a non-talker and no-nonsense law enforcement officer. He got to the point with precision and weight. Or he had, at least until he met and married his wife, Blake. The gossip about her had been more sensational than that about her husband.

She was a former sheriff, current law enforcement,

and wasn't afraid to let her braids down if needed—Mr. Donahue's daughter's words. Locals often joked about which one of the two won in arguments between the powerhouse hitters. Almost everyone eventually agreed it was Blake. She had won Weaver's heart completely, and together they had a blended family that was as loving as it was exciting.

Still, when it came to his work, it was heavily rumored that when Weaver stepped into the department wearing *that look*, no one could deny he was made to be sheriff.

James straightened his back a little as the man of the hour walked into the meeting room. He believed the rumors then.

Sheriff Weaver demanded attention without ever needing to steal it.

Rose had indulged him by letting James hold her elbow earlier, but now she was tip-top, sitting up tall in the seat next to him. Tall, for her at least. James pulled his glance at her up, up and away once the sheriff had settled at the head of the table. Then both were focused on the man with the shiny badge.

"Glad to see you up and moving in person, Rose, but, again, I wish you'd called one of us first before you left." The sheriff's tone was hard but James got the impression there was affection wrapped in it too.

James felt a little tap on the arm closest to her. Rose played off both stern and concerned with a simple shrug.

"Being discharged just timed right with Mr. Keller here's lunch delivery," she said. "I was going to call once I was back home."

The sheriff's gaze swung to James.

He gave Weaver a small nod.

"That's nice of you," he noted.

James couldn't help it.

"You save me from a bomb, I'll make you a sandwich."

Neither law enforcement officer chuckled, smiled or commented on that little joke. Instead, both tensed in unison. Their eyes met and James realized he didn't like feeling left out.

He didn't have to sit with the emotion for too long.

"What's up, Liam?" Rose asked. "What happened while I was in the hospital? What did Darius find?"

James knew she was talking about Detective Darius Williams, the only detective in the McCoy County Sheriff's Department, but he hadn't seen the man yet. Instead, all questioning and statements had been handled by the sheriff and a bomb tech and specialist sent from some city unit to investigate the explosion. James had wondered if Darius was out of town or simply kept missing him.

Sheriff Weaver leaned forward. He pointed to James.

"Does him being in here with you mean you want him in here or do I need to escort him out?"

A flash of worry went through James. Then he felt a poke at his arm again.

"He's apparently my plus-one," she said. "You can just go ahead."

The sheriff nodded. That flash of worry ebbed and was replaced by focus.

Weaver domed his fingers together as he rested his hands on the tabletop and dove in.

"For once, we found out a lot," he started. "Instead of having to dig and dig to try and figure out the answer to a million mysteries all wrapped and tangled together, I think we actually have most of the facts now."

Rose's chair squeaked as she leaned forward. James knew he wasn't blocking her line of vision to the sheriff because of where Weaver was sitting, but still James instinctively rolled back a little.

"You mean you know who planted the bomb?" she asked. "And why?"

The sheriff didn't look like he wanted to nod but he did.

"Darius found one of the men who'd showed up at the garage before the bomb went off. He was hurt and suddenly very worried about life after death and the sins that might affect him after it was all said and done. He was…very forthcoming."

The sheriff sighed.

There was no more dancing around it.

"You were targeted, Rose," he said simply. "Him, and the three other men, were told to follow you but keep their distance. They were also instructed to call a number if anyone looked like they were going to get into your car's passenger seat. Then they were supposed to record a video. They didn't know about the bomb, though, and only called the man who contracted them when they realized you were headed to the mechanic's shop and figured he might have had something planned with the car itself. He was extremely surprised when the bomb went off and the four of them fled the moment they could."

James didn't realize his hand had curled into a fist until pain bit into his palm.

He didn't dare say anything.

It was Rose's show.

"Who hired them?" she asked. "And why my passenger's seat?"

The sheriff's jaw tensed. It seemed to pain him to bite out the name.

"It was Damon Tillman."

James didn't recognize the name, but Rose sure did. Her face seemed to drain of color. It was such a drastic change from what he was becoming used to that James reached his hand out under the table toward her.

His knuckles brushed the fabric of her sweatpants.

She didn't react to it.

"Damon Tillman," she repeated.

The sheriff nodded.

James waited for a follow-up explanation. The two of them simply stared in silence for a moment.

"Does anyone know where Damon is now?" Rose said after a moment.

Her calm voice grated on James. It didn't seem appropriate for the topic, especially not when the sheriff was making no show of hiding his own anger.

"No. That's what Darius has been doing. Trying to track him down. Four men were working for him and apparently not one of them can point us in any one direction. We just know he's…around."

A knock on the door timed eerily with his last words.

A woman with long braids and a very pregnant belly walked in after he called out. Her expression softened slightly as she swung a smile to him and Rose before her gaze fell on Weaver.

"I'm sorry for the interruption, but I need to see you for a minute," she told him.

Sheriff Weaver seemed to split between alert and soft. He nodded.

"Excuse me," he told them.

James belatedly recognized the woman as Blake, the sheriff's wife, after they left.

That, in itself, was a feat considering his attention was so fully wrapped around whatever it was that Rose *wasn't* saying.

Once the door was closed and it was just the two of them, James couldn't stop himself. He fanned his hand out onto the thigh of Rose's pants and patted twice.

"What's up?" he asked. "Who is Damon Tillman?"

Rose stared straight ahead. She sighed out short.

"A consequence," she said. "Mine, actually."

James raised his eyebrow.

"Your consequence? For what?"

James kept his hand on her as the woman with a big attitude seemed to become incredibly small. He didn't understand it. He didn't like it.

If there had been more time, James might have taken a moment to wonder why he had gone from knowing *of* Wildcard Rose Little to *needing* to know her in such a short amount of time.

But, for the moment he was in, he gave all thoughts to her.

Rose shook her head. Pain contorted her face.

"For hesitating."

Chapter Seven

Five months earlier

The first tornado touched down between the county lines. It triggered one of the two sirens in Seven Roads to blare. Rose barely heard the commotion. She was with Doc Ernest in the hospital, looking at the good doctor's phone alongside Doc-Ernest-in-training, Lily.

"I knew they said the weather was going to get bad, but I didn't think we'd get tornadoes on top of flash flooding," Lily said to her mother. Doc Ernest simply shrugged.

"We had a hurricane hit us all the way here a few years back and no one predicted that would rock us like it did," she pointed out. "Like people, in the end predicting weather seems to come down to fate."

Rose, standing between them in plain clothes, didn't know about the fate part but she agreed that being caught off guard by the difference in a weather forecast and the actual weather that showed up wasn't so rare.

The severity had been slightly jarring, though. If she had known it would turn out like this, she would have spent her off time at home and not taken the drive out across the county.

Rose snaked her hand around to Doc Ernest's phone and turned the volume up. She had known the woman since they were toddlers—she'd actually babysat the college-age Lily back when the girl was small. That wasn't all that uncommon for the career locals of Seven Roads. They were born together, grew up together and aged together. They also attended all the big events together, whether they wanted to or not. Price had once called it trauma bonding. Sometimes, Rose didn't disagree.

"It sounds like this tornado is heading away from here and town. Also—given the debris tracker..." Rose tilted her head a little as the meteorologist tracked the radar live. "Yeah, I don't think that's messing up any houses or businesses. That's mostly field and trees up until County Road 72. Hopefully it winds down before it gets to the roads."

Doc Ernest and Mini Doc Ernest nodded in agreement. They had each been through a tornado or two before. There was no reason to panic until there *was* a reason to panic.

"I still bet your sheriff is getting a call or two," the older woman told Rose. "That flooding is probably washing out Mrs. Glenn's driveway and front lawn. That, plus the sirens, and I wouldn't be surprised if she hadn't already sounded her own alarms. That woman could be sitting dry and safe and she's still going to call for one of McCoy County's finest to come keep her company."

"That's only because her no-good son up and left her alone after he skipped town with his mistress," Lily pointed out. "I'd be calling for company too if I was her."

Her mother gave her the side-eye.

"Gossip doesn't become you, Miss Ernest. Not even the juicy kind."

Lily disagreed and the two devolved into a mother-daughter bickering. Rose took the opportunity to step away. She considered calling the sheriff to see if he did in fact need some help before Price's ID popped up on the phone instead.

"Hey, Wildcard, are you at home relaxing?" Price said in lieu of a greeting. He was obviously outside. The wind tore through his speakers. Rose pulled the phone away from her ear a little.

"No, I came out to eat with Doc Ernest for lunch at the—"

"Are you at the hospital?" he interrupted, volume going up a few notches.

Rose nodded to no one.

"Yeah. I got here before the weather went wonky. Why?"

"This is fate, I tell you what," Price said. "We got a call for help from those Camden people and, wouldn't you know it, they're outside of the hospital's new research annex."

There was that talk of fate again. Though the coincidence was there. The research annex was on the back end of the hospital's lot, a quick drive on a service road away from where she was now.

It was surprising to Rose that the "Camden people"—the staff running the drug trials for Camden Pharmaceuticals—were asking for help. The research annex had received all kinds of grants and funding to become a gem-in-the-wild, top-notch building. The staff inside had been rumored to have all glowing résumés too.

Price, however, was quick to explain the reason why the building's integrity didn't matter.

"Those workers are all from up North and none of them know how to handle tornado weather," he continued. "So, instead of hunkering down, they panicked when they heard the first of the sirens start up. They tried to take their shuttle up to the hospital. Now it sounds like they got stranded on the road that runs between the annex and the county."

Rose gave a silent wave to the doc and her daughter and headed for the elevators.

"Are there any injuries?"

Rose could bring help to them if needed, but Price told her no.

"Nope, but there are eleven of them. And it sounds like they're panicking. The bus blew a tire and that put them snug in a ditch. We had a car headed that way, but the flooding is slowing us down. I called on the off chance you were wild enough to be driving around in this weather. And look at this, you're now definitely the one closest to them. Is your badge on you?"

Rose confirmed it was in her car. When she was buckled inside a minute later, she threw the lanyard it was on around her neck.

"One of us should be to y'all soon," Price said as they were ending the call. "Stay safe, Wildcard. And watch the weather. The air still feels weird."

They didn't know how ominous those words would

later become. Instead, the call dropped, and Rose drove the service road attached at the back of the lot and headed toward the new, fancy, research annex.

She didn't make it far without stopping.

There were only two ways to get to the high-tech annex—the road from the hospital and the road from the county. Both converged for a three-way stop surrounded by trees. Rose understood why the bus had been stranded on the road leading to the hospital. There was a tree down, blocking the road near the three-way.

She stopped her car and jumped out to survey the damage.

The road was almost impassable, completely so for a bus. For her old car? Rose decided she could make it work. And she did. Slowly and with great caution, she maneuvered the flooded shoulder until she cleared the debris. The parking lot of the annex hadn't fared too much better. It was partially flooded and mostly covered in leaves and branches that had been stripped from the surrounding trees.

There was no bus, so she backtracked and went the only direction she could.

The road to the county was as country as they came. Dirt and gravel and underbrush creeping out. Trees lining the sides and some old fence, from the property of an owner who had long since passed on, scattered between. Not exactly a wooded area but enough oaks to shade the road even when the sun was in the sky.

Rose knew the road.

The one she stared at now was unrecognizable.

The hours of rain had seemed to collect solely in this area. She could only see patches of the dirt and gravel beneath the water. She bet that was why the bus had driven where it shouldn't have. Instead of being within the lanes, it was on the shoulder, sitting at an odd angle.

The back emergency door was open and facing her.

That was when she first saw Lloyd Harrison.

Tall, thin, and wearing an outfit that seemed to come right out of a movie—white lab coat, comically large ID badge and booties still wrapped around the bottoms of his shoes—he looked nothing but flustered as he yelled out to Rose when she stepped out onto the only part of the road that hadn't yet been submerged.

"We can't move," he cried, his voice carrying through the wind. "Our front tire blew, and we can't drive out of whatever we're stuck in!"

Rose assumed he had already spotted her badge hanging around her neck but motioned to it all the same.

"I'm a deputy with the McCoy County Sheriff's Department," she yelled out. "I'm here to help! Right now, let's sit tight and figure—"

Rose's words were strangled by a sound that made her blood run cold.

A tornado siren.

It tore through the air with an eerie echo.

Screams exploded from the bus.

"Keep calm," she instructed. "Just because it's going off doesn't mean it's near us! It just means it's in the county."

To help her point, Rose pulled her phone up and went to the local weather station's social media page. She clicked on their meteorologist's live feed, ready to prove to the panicked people on the bus that they had time to make good decisions. That this new threat was scary, but not something they had to deal with themselves.

The meteorologist's face filled her screen, focused and commanding, a map of McCoy County beneath his waving arms.

He spoke and Rose heard him, yet, months later, but she still wouldn't remember what he actually said. Instead, all her attention had stuck to the red area on the map he seemed to be so concerned about.

It turned out Rose was wrong.

It looked like they didn't have much time to make good decisions at all.

So she worked with what she had.

Rose flung herself back into the car and hit the gas. Her old car lurched into the rushing floodwaters with absolute obedience. If it had been higher, she couldn't have done it. And if she hadn't been so small herself, rolling down the driver's-side window and crawling up onto the roof of her car would have been harder. As it was, she managed both actions in rapid succession. The metal roof held sturdy as she found her balance and turned to face a wide-eyed Lloyd Harrison. Now there was only the space of her hood between her and him at the back emergency exit.

Rose kept her voice as calm as possible. She also made it as loud as possible too.

"Jump down here, climb over the car and run as soon as you hit the ground," she yelled, the siren continuing to wail in the background. "Whoever has the keys to the annex go first. We need to take shelter *now*!"

If there had been only a few people stranded on the bus, then she would have found a way to get them in her car to drive away. But true to what Price had said, there were eleven people crowded inside.

Their best bet was to use her car as a bridge and then run like there was no tomorrow back to the research annex.

She hoped.

Lloyd must have agreed. One glance at the water still going strong around the bus and he was shouting for someone behind him.

A second later a small woman appeared in the doorway.

Speed was the name of her game. She was on the hood of Rose's car with keys held high on her hands.

"I—I have the keys," she huffed out, scrambling to Rose's outstretched hand. When they connected, she pulled the woman easily up the windshield.

"The water isn't as deep behind the car," Rose said, pointing to the area just past the trunk. "Be careful and haul ass once you're down!"

The sound of wind combined with an eerie humidity in the air. The radar played on repeat in the back of Rose's mind. There was a tornado on the tracker…and that tracking hadn't been that far away from their road.

The tornado could still turn, though.

It could still dissipate.

It could—

The sound of snapping trees sounded in the distance.

Rose couldn't see past the bus but there was no ignoring the new urgency.

The people on the bus seemed to feel it too.

Up until then Rose had never met any of the Camden Pharmaceutical staff, and while their storm-panic was the reason they were all out there now, she had to admit once the crisis had a clear plan, they executed it with surprising efficiency.

Lloyd funneled people around him and down onto the car, Rose helped them over the windshield and roof, and an older woman named Claudia stood in the water just past the trunk, helping those through the transition to the non-flooded part of the road.

Once the Camden people's feet found solid ground? They ran like the devil was on their heels.

Which, maybe he was.

Rose heard the horribly familiar sound of a tornado headed their way.

They were out of time.

"We have to go," she yelled up at Lloyd. "*Now!*"

Lloyd disappeared back into the bus.

Rose was dumbstruck.

A heartbeat went by.

Then another.

It was too much.

"Hey!" she yelled, but her words were ripped up into the cacophony of sounds bearing down on them.

What happened to him?

Rose couldn't just wait around to find out.

Adrenaline coursing through her veins, she slid down the windshield and made quick work of shuffling to the edge of the car hood. She could now see into the bus.

That was when she first saw Derrick Tillman.

Unlike Lloyd, he was on the shorter side and not at all lean. He was muscular—tattoos lined the muscles visible from the short-sleeved shirt he wore with jeans. He was undeniably younger than Lloyd.

And he was also undeniably much angrier than the man.

"Hey!" Rose yelled.

Neither man seemed to listen to her as Derrick lunged down the aisle at Lloyd.

They were shouting but she couldn't hear exactly what they were saying.

She thanked years of exercise and somewhat decent balance and threw herself up and through the emergency exit. By the time she was standing inside of the bus, the men were already exchanging hits.

"Stop," she ordered, closing the space between her and the scuffle. "What are you guys doing? We have to go!"

Lloyd was closer, so Rose used every bit of her strength to pull him backward first. The move worked and he groaned as he broke from the fight and hit the floor.

The bus lurched in tandem with the power shift.

Rose yelled back to Lloyd to run.

This time, he listened.

Derrick, however, swayed.

Rose's interference in the fight had left him off-balance. He was going to fall. Rose, the only person left behind, started to reach out on reflex.

But that was when she saw it.

That was when she saw his face.

His expression.

His...rage.

And it made her pause.

It was a brief whisper of a moment. The space between two breaths.

Yet, it made all the difference.

Derrick hit the ground. Rose reached for him again. She hooked her arm around his, and pulled him up. It was a sloppy attempt made even more awkward by the disparity in their sizes. Still, they stood and started moving.

Rose was at the opening first and let go to drop down onto the hood of her car. Lloyd was still there. He reached out to steady her but she was turning around to face the bus, her hand already outstretched.

But the bus wasn't there.

And neither was Derrick Tillman.

Now

ROSE SHIFTED. JAMES SAW it in the change of her posture as she came to the ending of the story. He felt it beneath his hand too. Like her body had given in to absolute and unwavering defeat.

That defeat was punctuated by a voice he wouldn't have recognized as belonging to the wildcard deputy, had he not been looking at her lips as she spoke them.

"The tornado barely missed us, but it was close enough that the damage was severe," she wrapped up. "The bus and the trees around it never stood a chance. Along with the floodwaters, it went from right there to—" Her gaze seemed to hollow. She let out a breath and continued the thought. "—to over a hundred yards away. Lloyd and I were lucky. He pulled us into my car and the only damage it took was a cracked window from debris. That's why everyone became so obsessed with my car. It survived a flood and tornado, but not the bus."

Rose's voice deflated to complete lifelessness.

"And not Derrick either. Once the dust had settled, we found Derrick. He was still inside the bus. He didn't make it."

James watched as the usually animated woman seemingly shut down completely. Without her saying it, he knew she was done with the story. Not only done now but maybe would never tell again.

Still, he felt the need to make some points he felt she was missing.

"Derrick's death wasn't your fault," he underlined first. "Unless Wildcard Rose has some tricks up her sleeve that I don't know about, you can't control the weather and that goes doubly for the bad parts. In fact, it seems to me that you could have left anytime. Instead, you stayed. You thought quick, acted quicker, and gave those people a chance."

James applied pressure down on her thigh. He used it and his hand to turn the rest of her body around with the chair.

Rose's eyes were dark. They also felt warm. James stared into them now, head-on.

"Your car could have stalled or been swept away. But you made it a bridge. Those fully grown adults could have figured it out from there—jump on the car, cross the worst part of the water, and run back to cover—but you stayed. You held hands so feet could move easier. You kept calm so others had more space to panic. You jumped into a worse situation and tried to make sure everyone came with you when it was time to go."

James didn't know Rose well enough to keep touching her—he knew this in the back of his mind, the same thought when he had first touched her leg—but now he wasn't sure how else to get through to her.

So he moved his hand to the side of her face.

It was so small in his palm.

"Loss always hurts. No matter if it was by your hand or not." He tilted his head a little and also smiled a little. "I saw the recording that the Camden lady took of you helping them off the bus. But I wonder if you ever watched it. All of it, I mean?"

He wasn't surprised that Rose shook her head to that. She didn't seem the type to watch something people praised as being her heroic moment. Especially when all she saw was the loss of Derrick.

"She was still recording when they made it back to the annex. It was mainly just sounds of the storm and sirens and panic *but* if you listen carefully, you can hear someone getting a call out in the background. It was to their mom. They said they were scared but that it was okay too. Because help had shown up."

He ran his thumb along her cheekbone and upped his smile.

"You risked your life to try and give eleven people a better chance at surviving a wild and awful situation, Little," he said. "One person sadly didn't make it. Ten people did. And *that* is why everyone fell in love with this story. It's incredible. Just like you."

James hadn't meant to say the last part. Or really, he hadn't known he was going to say it.

Yet, it seemed right.

So he let the words sit between them without scrambling to erase them.

He wasn't sure if Rose would let them sit for long and he didn't get a chance to see what she would do or say.

The door to the conference room opened. James dropped his hand and turned to see Sheriff Weaver looking ten kinds of angry.

He said four words.

They packed one hell of a punch.

"We have a problem."

Chapter Eight

Rose had grown up in Seven Roads. Born there, gone through childhood there, and had only left for school before coming right on back. She was as tried and true a local as Price, with roots just as deep as those of Liam's wife, Blake. And even though her parents had moved to Tennessee five years prior, and her aunt and cousin had followed them too, she wasn't short on people she could count on in a pinch.

Yet, there she was accepting help from James like she had no other options in the bag.

"I already got your shop blown up, so are you sure you want me hanging out with you?" she asked, half joking, half absolutely serious. The man had already gone through a few inches with her, now she was asking for some miles.

James shrugged the question off.

"I'm the one who offered first," he pointed out. "If you're so worried, make me sign a waiver." He cracked a smile then pointed past the windshield to a building coming into view in the distance. They had been driving for at least fifteen minutes since leaving the sheriff's department. Rose knew the area but hadn't before seen the house James had moved into since coming to Seven Roads years ago.

Not that she was sure what she was looking at was a home.

James chuckled, maybe picking up on her thoughts.

"Plus, some days I think it might be easier to just start over with this heap anyways," he said. "Having it blow up might help me more than it hurt me." He let his foot up on the gas and maneuvered them into a gravel parking spot. It cornered an open field of overgrown grass. It wasn't as wide or vast as Old Man Becker's fields on the opposite side of town, but it took some squinting to see the furthest edge near a cropping of trees off in the distance.

James put the truck in Park, puffed out his chest and made sure she was looking at him before he spoke clearly and with ample volume.

"Unless I'm in there when it blows. If that's the case, I hereby absolve you of any guilt, Rose Little." He held up three fingers like he was making a Scouts' honor sign. "I, James Keller of sound mind, invited you to my home of my own doing. Anything and everything that happens after this point was because I'm a ten-out-of-ten individual with nerves of steel and a kind, caring heart. Oh, and charming too. And funny. And a mechanic whiz."

Rose snorted.

"And apparently humble."

He gave her a thumbs-up.

"See? You understand how outstanding I am. So let's just stop this whole 'stay away' bit you've been trying to pull since Sheriff Weaver came into that room with the whole 'good news, bad news' thing." James, dare she think it, turned almost sulky. "I have to be honest though, I thought that had become our trauma-bond thing."

Rose felt her eyebrow rise at his expression, but he was already going about getting out of the truck to catch it.

James was a big, intimidating man.

He was also surprisingly childlike at times.

It was almost refreshing.

Especially after the news Liam had given them back at the department.

"The good news is we just found the bomb maker," Liam had said after stepping back into the conference room. "His name is Dave Kyler and one of the men who came to the garage at Damon's order was the one to roll on him. Darius, along with the FBI agent who came in once a bomb was in play, found Dave not too far from here. They're still talking to him, but Darius said so far it looks like he was given a pretty penny to assemble it."

Rose hadn't recognized the name but was relieved that the one with the ability to make homemade bombs might be truly out of the picture.

"And the bad news?" she had to ask.

Liam had put his hands on his hips. Another big-man gesture in contrast with his icy exterior.

"He said the original plan was to put it in your apartment, but he refused, because even though he saw you as a job, he didn't want to hurt any kids."

"Melinda and Madeline," Rose offered.

Liam had nodded, not at all happy.

James had spoken up then, to ask, "Melinda and Madeline?"

"The children of the family in the unit across the hall from my apartment."

"Which is the bad news," Liam had said.

Rose had agreed, but still she had to say it out loud. "It means that Damon definitely knows where I live."

That one statement had led her to the beginning of a cracked concrete path that ran straight to a house that looked as frustrated and tired as she felt.

The man who owned the weathered two-story house was opposite it in cheer. Smiling once again, he waved his arm out toward the worn brick and made an exaggerated announcement.

"Wildcard Little, welcome to the purchase I'll probably never financially recover from."

James led her down the path and into the house without any more fanfare. Rose split her attention between her surroundings and the man next to her as they walked through each room. No one was hiding or ready to attack during the first-floor tour of the kitchen, dining room, living area, laundry room, or bathroom. The same held true for the upstairs. James gave a flourish when they made it to the guest bedroom she would be staying in for the near future.

It, like the bubbly personality that occasionally surfaced in its owner, was a surprising contrast to the work-in-progress look of the rest of the home. Everything was…soft. Soft on the eyes and seemingly to the touch. Even the small knickknacks and framed pictures on the walls had a feeling of warmth emanating from them.

This wasn't just a guest bedroom. It was a room that had been set up with extreme care and with a heavy feminine hand.

Was James just that good at design or had a woman helped him with this?

A question that Rose hadn't thought to ask until now blared across her mind.

Was… Was James in a relationship? His ring finger was bare but that didn't mean he wasn't taken.

How had she disrupted this man's life without knowing a thing about his life?

What if she wasn't just intruding in his life but also his—

"I know what you're thinking," James said, setting her hospital bag on top of the vanity next to the bed and interrupting her internal spiral. "Normally, I should get some kind of HGTV award for this little oasis, but I'm sad to say, this was all Mom."

Rose's worries skidded to a halt.

"Your mom?" she repeated.

He nodded.

"She said she didn't care how long it takes me to fix this place up as long as I have a nice place for company," he said. "I think she was meaning that more for her than anyone else. She wasn't exactly a fan of me buying this heap."

In a rare change, James seemed to express a feeling of doubt.

"To be honest, I hadn't really planned on it either."

He sighed and switched back to the tour in the span of a breath.

"The bathroom in the hallway is nice too and my room is on the other side of it down the hall. Feel free to roam anywhere. This place may not look the greatest but it's functional and safe. You won't go falling through any holes in the ceiling or accidentally use pipes that will spray water everywhere."

"Ah, the two movie pitfalls of renovating," she said with humor.

James shrugged.

"You laugh, but my first month here?" He pulled a blank expression. "Both happened."

That lack of emotion wiped away with a laugh. One Rose shared in.

It blocked the reality of their present predicament for a while. James excused himself to let her get settled and took a phone call somewhere else in the house. Rose used his absence to her advantage and called her parents.

Hiding what had happened with the bomb had been impossible once it hit the local news, never mind the gossip. Rose had known this impossibility would back her into a corner, so she had been preemptive and come out swinging before that happened. She had called her parents as soon as the first doctor had spoken to her once she had woken up in the hospital.

The Littles weren't totally gobsmacked that Rose had found herself in another dangerous situation. They were, however, very reactive to the fact that this time around there had been an explosion.

"Seven Roads is supposed to be a sleepy town, but I swear all you seem to be getting is nightmares!" her mom had exclaimed once she realized Rose was fine. "We can find you a better life here. One that isn't this—this dangerous!"

Her father had been less loud. And demanding.

"She's not wrong, Rosy. You have to admit your last

few tumbles in Seven Roads have been pretty spectacular. Not in a good way, either."

"Which means I should be good from here on out," Rose had tried to assure them. "I've been through the extreme parts, now we should be at the boring, paperwork ones."

It was a lie.

But Rose had never been against telling a fib or two to ease the worries of loved ones. Loved ones who could be used against her if they came back to town to see about her. A point Rose had to underline to her father without admitting that Damon Tillman was still out there and probably would still be gunning for her.

"Hey, Dad, there's a few people still not the happiest with me and I'm worried some of that could reach up to y'all. So do me a favor and keep a good eye out there. Maybe even stay close to the house until things have cooled off around here."

Her father, ever a girl dad, seemed to be caught between talking to his baby girl and talking to the strong, independent woman he had helped raise.

"Will do," he had eventually promised. "You keep us in your loop, Rosy. Texts, if not calls, every day to let us know you're good. Put the code in it too so I know no one's messing with us."

Rose had smiled at that. She had grown up watching spy thrillers, police procedurals and action flicks with her parents. One day they had joked they needed a family code to use just in case. That joke had turned into an all-out family tradition between the three of them.

Now, sitting at a small table in the kitchen downstairs, Rose sent off a quick follow-up text telling her dad that she loved them.

She added the word *hon* at the end.

It was only by the grace of good reflexes that she kept from jumping when James appeared by her shoulder and repeated the last word.

"*Hon?*" One syllable but it came out strong and deep.

Rose flipped her phone over onto the tabletop and crossed her arms over her chest with a scowl. One that was definitely heating.

"Well, aren't we nosy."

James held up his hands in defense as he walked over to the refrigerator.

"I wasn't meaning to be," he said. "My eyes tend to wander when my feet are." He did his Scouts' honor sign again. "No disrespect meant."

Rose believed him, so she answered his question. Though she did it with the scowl still hanging on. She might have realized she was more comfortable with the man than was normal for her, but that didn't mean *he* had to know that too.

"It's from a show me and my parents watched a few years back during Christmas. It means 'honey.' If we don't say it, it's not us."

Other people might have had an eyebrow to raise at that, but James was simple.

He nodded with total acceptance.

"That's weirdly loving, Little. I bet your boyfriend gets a kick out of it too."

If Rose had been drinking something, she would have sputtered a little into it at that.

"If I were dating someone, they sure aren't hitting

the mark. Have you seen anyone around me?" She motioned to the empty room around them. "I may be wild but even I deserve someone who will show up when someone's trying to kill me."

It was an offhand comment. One that hadn't meant much to her.

Yet, it seemed to have struck some kind of a chord with James.

His smile left.

His words drove a stake into the ground.

"I'm here."

That heat from earlier expanded within Rose. She tried to play it off again, but this time, it didn't land as cleanly.

"I—I meant someone other than you. And well, the department." She forced a laugh. "Though I guess that's already more people than most get, so I shouldn't complain."

He was too far away for her to see the gold in his eyes, but the green grabbed her easy.

If he wanted to say something, he looked like he changed his mind in the middle of the thought. He shook his head a little.

Then that smile was back.

Suddenly, the small room felt much smaller with just the two of them in it.

And the heat in Rose's cheeks continued to simmer for it.

"THEY FOUND DAVE KYLER," the man said. "He was quick to admit you hired him to put a bomb in the deputy's apartment."

He was short but intimidating in his own right, clean-cut in his pressed, button-up and slacks, and hair styled with gel more expensive than most people's monthly paycheck. He was young too.

Not as young as Derrick had been.

Damon Tillman felt the rage in him pulse.

He didn't let it show. He had expected this news.

"Which means the deputy should have realized that I know where she lives now," Damon said. "Which means, if she's crafty, she'll find somewhere else to lay her head tonight." He felt the corners of his lips lift into sharp points. "And thankfully, she's as crafty as I hoped."

The young man opposite him, holding a clipboard and a blank expression like it was his only job in life, nodded.

"Not all of the guns for hire turned on you, but two did and that was enough," he added.

Damon nodded.

"Which already confirmed to that dear Detective Williams and sheriff that I'm still most likely in the area code."

The man agreed with his own nod. Then, despite his steely demeanor, he let some of the curiosity he'd been holding on to the last few months slip out.

"Why can't we do away with her now? We know where she is. It would be easy."

Damon felt like his smile was a knife, cutting into his own skin while it waited to cut into another's.

"Because Rose Little's being dead isn't the goal," he said. "It's the act of dying that I want to focus on."

The young man didn't ask any more questions. Instead, he gave the last of his report.

"Then I'll give Mr. Danvers the go-ahead."

Damon gave a slow nod.

"Even if she can survive this round, I doubt she will the next."

The young man left, but Damon stayed in the office.

While Rose's death by Mr. Danvers would work for him, Damon couldn't help but find himself rooting for Rose just a little.

Mr. Danvers would be quick.

What came next, wouldn't be.

Chapter Nine

James made a mean everything-omelet, filled with bacon and peppers, onions and two types of cheeses. It was his go-to meal, and had been since he was a teen. Now, as a man past thirty, wearing a set of coveralls and living in a house he had bought with money he'd earned with his hands, the meal felt different somehow.

Maybe because the first person he had served it to outside of his family had not only praised it, but asked for seconds.

It was more than satisfaction for him. It was a point of pride. A pride he wore with a growing smugness as he cleared the plates and handed her the coffee she had requested.

"I could get used to this," Rose muttered, taking the coffee with a nod. "You could turn this place into a bed-and-breakfast with your kind of service."

James laughed at that. He motioned to the peeling wallpaper in the corner and then the extremely outdated countertops and appliances.

"I'm not sure many people would want to vacation here, never mind in Seven Roads. We're not exactly a tourist trap."

"Hey, don't forget the power of passers-through, especially with the motel being out of business now." She shrugged. "A little paint here and there and I could see this place working."

James started to fix his own coffee. It was more a reflex than a need. Since offering Rose a place to stay he hadn't had any trouble staying awake.

"Sadly, my plans for this place aren't as grand as all that. I just want somewhere to grow roots, house some kids, and drive me a little crazy as we both age. I don't need outsiders trying to pay me to be nice."

Rose made a noise into her coffee. James turned with an eyebrow raised.

"What, are you surprised the big ol' mechanic man bought a house specifically for future kids?" he asked.

Rose put her coffee down and shook her hands in front of her.

"Not surprised you want to, just surprised how casual you were about saying it, is all. But maybe that's because I'm so used to getting asked when I'll get married and settle down that I'm a bit quiet on the topic."

James leaned against the counter. He knew it wasn't exactly his business, but he was curious.

"*Do* you want to get married and settle down?"

He half expected a glare or a pointed barb sent in his direction at the intrusion. Instead, he was met with a shrug.

"It's not off the table," she said. "I just haven't sat down at the table it's on yet, so to speak." She let out a sigh. He wondered if her head still hurt but decided to hold that question for later. Unlike this one, he wasn't sure she would be as honest with her answer. Admitting she was in pain didn't seem to be Rose Little's strong suit.

"The last guy I dated wasn't a fan of my job and—while I get that it's not for everyone and I don't blame those who stay away—he kept waiting for me to change my mind and leave the department. Leave Seven Roads. I'm not sure if he wanted the whole white picket fence thing but I know he didn't want me wearing a badge." Her hand moved beneath his sightline under the table. Like she was reaching for her badge on memory alone.

She lifted her gaze back to his. Her smile felt watered down but nonetheless sincere.

"I know I can belong other places but it's here where I *want* to belong," she finished.

James understood her, if only for different reasons. Since Rose had given him some information, he decided to share in kind.

"I had the opposite problem with my ex," he started. "She wanted me to stay in there and I wanted to be in Seven Roads. She didn't want a house of kids, and I don't think I could live in a house without them." James ran a hand across the back of his neck. "Though I've gotten a little off-track since helping Dad with the shop. Or maybe it sounds nicer to use your 'not at the right table yet' analogy. I'm not even sure I'm in the right room as my table yet."

As he said it, he couldn't help but notice that Rose was sitting at a very real table in his very real home. On the one hand, it was surreal. On the other, it felt oddly normal.

Rose's brow drew in. She voiced her question next.

"I don't know if it's impolite for me to ask but why

did you want to live in Seven Roads? You only lived here for a few years when you were a kid, right? Then came back a few years ago to start the shop? Why?"

This wasn't an unexpected question. James had been asked some variation of it more than a dozen times. Why had the kid with no true hometown come back to plant a flag, so to speak, in a place that he'd barely lived in before?

James pushed off the counter's edge and closed the space between them in two steps. He took her hand.

"Let me show you."

The land the old house sat on was just over one acre. It included the field and a cropping of trees just beyond it. That field of tall, wild grass looked the same as it had when he was six. Decades later and in the dying sunlight.

"When I was six, I got into a really big fight in a foster home I was staying at. It was a bad one too. I got hurt pretty good, landed myself in the hospital, and pretty much scared myself off people too. The county agency decided it would be better to shift me to a new place and, after a lot of back and forth, I landed in Seven Roads."

They were standing on the back porch, which was surprisingly not as worn as the rest of the home. James had dropped Rose's hand after they had gone through the back door, and now placed his own on the railing. The solid wood railing showed the remnants of stain long-since perfect.

He patted it once and with absolute affection.

"This was my last foster home before I went to the

Kellers but that's not why I bought this place. Want to see the real reason?"

Where he expected a little resistance, he received none. Instead, Rose let him take her hand again and this time lead her out into the tall grass. The fading light almost perfectly matched his memory as they walked through the overgrown back lot at a light pace.

Not too far from the house James stopped them and turned back around.

He dropped her hand and sighed out long.

That feeling was back, just as it always was when he was here.

And that was what James wanted to explain to Rose, for whatever reason.

"I was standing about right here when my mom called out to me that it was time to leave," he said. "Dad had just packed the last of my things I'd left behind and my aunt was helping my foster family tie up loose ends. *I* was out here, running around, because I was never really big on saying bye to a place. And honestly, I think I was still nervous I'd be left behind again."

James felt Rose's gaze on him, but he kept his stare locked onto the memory. He pointed to the back porch.

"But then Mom came out there and said it was time to go home. And she didn't move until I ran all the way from here to there." James looked at the distance between him and that porch. If there was ever one stretch of land he knew better than the rest, this small run was it. "My life changed in that next house—the house I ended up growing up in—but *this* is where my little world actually changed. It's the first time I felt like I was running toward something worth running for. So when I saw it was up for sale, I came back here with Dad to check it out. And wouldn't you know it, all I had to do was stand right here and that feeling came right on back."

He gave out a self-deprecating laugh.

"So I bought the house for this one piece of land as a gift to that scared and anxious seven-year-old. We made it! It was scary and stressful sometimes, but we made it all the same."

James knew it sounded cheesy, like some kind of movie that had a lot of crying and sharing of feelings, but it was all true.

Standing in the field and looking back at the house in the distance, lights on and warm against the approaching night, was a comfort. Plain and true.

A comfort he had never shared with anyone before, he realized.

Finally, he looked over at Rose.

She was facing the house now. Her hair was cute, held up in a messy bun at the nape of her neck. James bet she might tease him for his dramatic take on the dirt and grass they were standing on. However, Rose was frowning. Even in profile, it was pronounced.

"What's wrong?" he asked.

Her voice was nothing but agitation.

"You brought me—the lady who already got your workplace blown up—to a place *this* special and irreplaceable?" She whirled around to face him. Her hands went right to her hips like she was a teacher scolding a disappointing student. "Are you kidding me? Thanks for the pressure there, Mr. Keller!"

For a second, James worried that she was seriously mad. But then she rolled her eyes at him.

"Now I'm going to be worried about protecting you, me and an entire house," she continued.

James couldn't help but smile at how exasperated she sounded, especially when she started to walk back to the house, still complaining.

"I thought it was just some silly old house you got because the housing market is horrible," she continued. "But *noooo*. It's so sentimental that it made my heart squeeze. Ugh. Now I definitely need to find Damon as soon as possible."

James's smile softened as he watched the little Little stomp her way back toward the house with fake outrage.

He waited until she was a few steps away. Like he always did, James imagined his seven-year-old self running ahead, stomach knotted up in barely suppressed excitement.

That didn't change as he started to walk now.

This time, though, there was definitely something different.

This time he had someone to follow.

THERE WAS NO news from Liam, Detective Williams, or anyone else in the next few hours. It made Rose more anxious than if there had been something to report on, bad or not. Instead, she whittled the time away by pacing James's living room, being told by James not to pace in his living room, and by going back to pacing in James's living room.

He put the TV on and managed to sidetrack her for

a while but eventually Rose decided she needed something stronger than idle chatter.

So she took a bath.

The guest bathroom might have been dated but the tub was wide, deep and clean. There was even some fancy bubble bath mix beneath the sink, courtesy of James's mother, who—according to him—believed all baths should be drowning in bubbles. Rose didn't know if she agreed with it to that extent, but she poured in the lavender mix with the mindset of "when in Rome."

Thoughts about bubbles, bombs and Damon Tillman melted away as soon as Rose lowered herself into the hot water. The stress she had been carrying for days didn't go away but it had the peace of mind to pause.

Rose sighed out at the temporary relief.

Her thoughts floated around to simpler things. She wondered what she might have for breakfast the next day, what the weather might look like, about which house the couple on the TV show they had been watching ended up picking, and if James Keller took baths. Because, as she stretched her legs out and let her feet walk up the opposite end of the tub, she couldn't imagine a man as big as him fitting in one that wasn't extra-large.

She stayed with that image a little longer than she probably should have and then marveled at how ridiculous the last week or so of her life had gotten, from trying to get her car fixed to lounging in the mechanic's tub. She decided to never again judge another movie heroine who went from a normal life to a chaotic one so quickly.

Rose's thoughts doubled back to the man himself,

and the image of him standing next to her in the grassy field earlier. He had been so vulnerable, so honest, with his past that Rose hadn't known what to say—what to do. Putting on an act of being annoyed at trusting her around such a precious place was a last-second effort to remain unattached to his story.

But now she let her heart ache for him.

He had been through a lot and still found the bright side. A giant wall of an optimist wrapped in coveralls and muscle.

Rose started to smile, thinking about how he was still wearing his work coveralls, when a knock sounded on the door.

Her face instantly heated.

"Yeah?" she called.

The knock sounded again.

"I'm in the bath," she added, not that he should need reminding.

Rose imagined a sheepish grin on James's face on the other side of the door. Maybe he'd come to ask her if she needed anything or warn her about the old pipes or something.

But that knock came again.

Rose shifted in the bathwater, suddenly uncomfortable.

She eyed her phone on the counter, just out of arm's reach.

Maybe James was just messing with her.

Maybe he was just trying to scare her?

Even as she thought it, Rose knew that wasn't the case.

James might have acted childish on occasion, but

his manners were all well-behaved man. He wouldn't interrupt her privacy without a good reason.

That was why, without thinking, Rose hadn't locked the bathroom door.

And that was how, in what felt like slow motion, Rose watched that same door open.

Her opinion of James stayed true—he wasn't the type of man to invade her privacy and that was why she had felt safe.

But the man standing in the doorway now?

Good manners or not, he was no James Keller at all.

Chapter Ten

He looked like he had simply taken a turn down the wrong aisle at the grocery store after work. Everything about him was dress-code appropriate. His blond hair was neat and cut close, his outfit was a collared shirt tucked into khakis, and his shoes might have been sneakers, but they could definitely pass if he wore them out to church.

It wasn't just his clothes and hairstyle that gave the impression of office worker winding down from a long day, it was his looks that really sold the image well.

He was around Rose's age and boy-next-door handsome. Not so much that it made those around him gawk but enough to appreciate. He had all the angles and hard lines across his face and dark eyes that ran more rich than muddy. The rest of him was just as middle-of-the-road. He looked around average-height and build. His clothes fit him comfortably, not too snug.

This man, in all respects, was the neighbor you said hi to on walks or shared pleasantries with in the concession stand line of the local high school football games.

He looked…nice.

To Rose, he was utterly terrifying.

He cocked his head to the side and slid his hands into his pockets.

"You're Deputy Little." It wasn't a question.

Rose wanted to make sure he knew it was an answer regardless.

"I am a deputy with the McCoy County Sheriff's Department, yes."

The man kept his head on that tilt and scanned her and the tub. The bubbles she had contemplated earlier had thinned but it was enough to give her a little cover. Still, she internally squirmed at the look.

That squirm went right back to terror when he snorted.

"Congratulations, Deputy with the McCoy County Sheriff's Department." He straightened his neck and pulled his hands free from his pockets. "You'll be the first person I've ever drowned in a tub."

Rose was already moving, water sloshing as she scrambled to stand.

The man was just as quick.

He cut across the bathroom and grabbed her by the throat before she could get her legs beneath her. On reflex her hands went up to try and slip beneath his grip but her body was trying to do too many things at once. She couldn't get a finger beneath his hold, and she couldn't get her balance in the tub either. Both problems together created a new one as her feet slid out beneath her.

If she hadn't been so petite she believed the fight would have gone a little differently here, but as it was, the man easily followed her fall down alongside the tub. His hand stayed around her throat as he took a knee on the tile on the other side of the tub's edge. The air against Rose's chest and stomach was replaced by the warm water rushing back over her. She threw one hand out to stop her backward descent, but he still had one hand free.

He swatted it away with little difficulty.

"Don't worry. This might be my first time, but it will be fast."

He pushed down with the hand around her neck. She tried again to swing out at him, to claw him, to do something to his arm or face or anything.

But she was too small. Her opponent was too big. The disadvantage of being in the tub was too challenging.

Still, she wasn't simply going to lie there and take it without some pushback.

Rose lifted her leg and kicked out at the man's side.

The hit landed.

It wasn't enough to end the fight, but it was enough to make his grip on her slip.

Rose didn't waste time trying to stand again. She didn't waste breath trying to threaten him or plead with him. She didn't even use the precious few seconds to take a good, decent breath.

All the air left in Rose's lungs formed one thing and one thing only.

"James!"

No sooner had his name left her mouth than the intruder's efforts followed through. The calming bath with lavender bubbles turned into a burning nightmare. Rose thrashed around with her legs but couldn't get any real traction. She blindly beat at the man's arm with one hand while trying to pry free the other from around her neck.

She was so all-consumed with trying to shift him off her that realizing she couldn't breathe seemed to come last.

But it came with a quiet wallop.

Adrenaline and panic bloomed a field of screaming flowers within her, each one yelling something different.

She was Wildcard Rose and yet she was going to die in a bathtub.

Her parents were going to be devastated.

Who was this guy?

How had he gotten in?

Was James…?

Rose's head was pounding. Her chest burned. So did her eyes. She hadn't shut them despite the soap and water above her. The blurry image of the man to the side of the tub warped and moved.

That panic turned to rage.

At this man. At his audacity.

He might kill her, but she would leave her mark.

Rose always kept her nails short for work but when it came to a last act on Earth, they could still do the job. She heard the warbled cry of pain from the man as she used both hands to clamp onto his arm and dug her nails into his skin.

If he got away, they would be able to get his DNA from under her fingernails.

It was a small, shrinking thought as Rose started to lose the will to fight.

Her vision started to tunnel as a much smaller thought bubbled to the surface.

It was guilt.

The littlest Little would scar James's forever home with her death.

It wasn't a bomb in his shop, but it was a shame all the same.

She tried to picture James standing in that field earlier.

So peaceful.

The James who roared into the bathroom was not.

HE DIDN'T NEED any context. He didn't need any explanations or to ask any questions.

James Keller took in only one detail when he ran into the bathroom.

Some guy was hurting Rose.

That was all he needed.

James grabbed the man by the scruff of his shirt and yanked him with every bit of force he had. It was more than enough.

The man was a leaf on the wind as he flew backward and crashed onto his back on the tile. The impact pushed the air out of his lungs. More importantly, it freed Rose. Though she wasn't surfacing.

James closed the distance to the tub in two strides and plunged his arms into the water. In the next moment Rose was out and up against him.

The man behind him squelched against the tile. James spun around, Rose against his chest, and kicked the man hard. He was back against the tile and sliding toward the wall.

James would have done more, but if Rose wasn't breathing, then he—

Rose's body was wracked with coughing. She spluttered and gasped and slapped at her chest.

It was a beautiful sight.

One that spelled out his next step.

James ran out of the bathroom and dropped Rose onto the bed. She was still coughing as she looked up at him, red eyes wide.

"Phone's in my room," was all he said.

Then he went back into the bathroom and slammed the door shut behind him.

He locked it.

The man who had dared to lay a hand on Rose was getting to his feet.

His eyes widened too.

James smiled.

"I'm no unsuspecting woman in a bathtub but I sure hope you won't mind fighting me."

He didn't know if the man had a weapon hidden in his clothes but didn't give him a chance to grab for any. He was on the stranger in a few steps. He threw a hit the second he was close enough.

The man didn't dodge it, but he did block. That was the same for the next few hits James tried to land. He was hoping for a knockout punch but instead he was bruising the man's forearms and sides.

Which was fine by him.

They were still hits. He was still damaging the body, even if he wasn't hitting his target.

The man must have realized that too. He took a

chance and dropped low. James's fist hit empty air. It left an opening that allowed the other man to spring up and across at him.

His shoulder connected with James's ribs.

It made him stagger back.

The other man must have thought this was a winning move. The beginning to an end he surely wanted.

But James had been through worse in his life, even before the bomb in the auto shop.

His life had built him up to one truth.

He *endured.*

James tightened the muscles in his legs and did a move he had only ever seen used once. He left his face and chest open and grabbed each of the man's biceps in his hands. James pushed the man away from him but didn't let go.

It created obvious confusion in the assailant.

James gritted his teeth.

He didn't need to land a punch to knock someone out.

Instead, he could simply use his head.

And he did.

James slammed his head against the man's without mercy. The man could no more dodge the hit than he could block it. Pain exploded behind James's eyes and his vision spotted.

But he stayed standing.

The other man did not.

His body went limp in James's hands.

James let him drop the rest of the way to the tile floor.

It wasn't a knockout punch, but it would do.

James hesitated only long enough to make sure he wasn't getting back up and then hurried to unlock the door. He flung it open just in time to see a flurry of motion enter from his right.

His fist went up, ready to rumble with whoever the intruder had brought, but the source of the motion was the woman he was ready to rumble for.

Rose was wrapped in a sheet, still dripping wet from head to toe, and a phone pressed against her cheek. Soap bubbles were still scattered across her hair. They offset the severity of the red handprint around her neck.

"Are you okay? Where is he?" Her voice was hoarse. It made the anger in him mount again.

"I'm good," he answered. He thumbed over his shoulder. "He's out. For now. Do you have your cuffs with you?"

Rose relayed the details to whoever she was on the phone with but nodded to James. She pointed to her bag in the corner. James went through it with as much respect as possible, only lightly noting her handcuffs were tangled up with a pair of underthings.

"Behind his back," she instructed.

James could hear whoever was on the other side of the phone talking quick. Rose replied in kind, but he had moved too far away to hear exactly what. Instead, his focus moved to the man as he rearranged him to cuff his wrists behind his back.

Who was he?

Where had he come from?

James had been in the kitchen when he'd heard Rose yell for him. Before that he had been in the living room.

Both places gave him an easy view of the front and back doors. And even if they didn't, where he had been in each room had given him a clear sight line to the bottom of the stairs.

Had the man still managed to sneak by him?

Had he found a different way to the second floor?

Or had he already been in the house before Rose had gone upstairs?

If so, then why did he wait to attack her when she was in the bath?

James finished his task and sat back on the tile floor to face him.

His hit had busted the man's nose. Broken it, maybe. It was a mercy if that was all. James could have done a lot more.

Rose appeared at his side. Instead of sitting next to him where he had leaned back to rest on the tile, she pulled up on his elbow. Her hand was still wet. He let her lead him back out to the bedroom. She was no longer on the phone.

"The sheriff is on the way," she said. "I need to get dressed but I'm getting kind of uncomfortable at the thought of changing with him in there and someone maybe coming up the stairs."

James understood what she was asking. She'd stopped him at the one spot in the room where he could see the bathroom and into the hallway without having to turn toward each.

He nodded.

"I'll keep watch, you change."

“Thank you.” Her voice was still hoarse. It grated at James.

He couldn’t believe she had been attacked in *his* home.

He was supposed to protect her.

What if he hadn’t heard her?

What if he’d been too late?

The what-ifs were brutal. James tried to keep his anger from boiling over while Rose went out of his sight line behind him to dress.

“That’s not Damon.” The sound of sliding fabric was a background to a solid-sounding Rose. “If you were wondering,” she added. “I don’t recognize him at all.”

“Just like you didn’t recognize the men at the auto shop.”

“Just like I didn’t recognize the men at the auto shop,” she repeated.

There was strength in her voice, but that voice went quiet. So did James. Over a week of two attempts on her life, three counting the bomb, and there she was still standing. Not silent, not silenced.

James marveled at her resilience.

Even when he felt something against the middle of his back.

His mind was fast to stay his reflexes when he realized it was Rose. She was leaning against him, her forehead warm even through the back of his shirt.

He felt her sigh out more than he heard it.

There was no denying that it shook. So did her voice when she spoke.

“Good news, we survived another round. Bad news,

I—I think this round was a little too much for me. I—I might cry. C-can I stay here until they arrive?"

James knew she was already crying. He wasn't going to point it out.

Instead, he nodded.

"Do what you need to do, Wildcard. I'm not going anywhere."

Chapter Eleven

The Seven Roads Motel wasn't actually out of business. Instead, it was waiting in a limbo between the former owner and the one who was taking it over—his ex-wife. Her name was Brandy Lane, and she was the disowned granddaughter of the Lanes whom the hospital was named after.

She was also close friends with Detective Darius Williams, one of the few people in the sheriff's department who knew about what had happened at James's home.

And knew that Rose and James were now about to stay at that motel. Room 6, to be exact.

"Brandy's no-good ex is living in Texas now, so he won't barge in here asking questions or anything," Darius explained. "Not that he cares about the property. He just wanted to tie Brandy up in legal fees and paperwork before she could open it back up."

He helped them into the room and, along with James, was inspecting every inch. Rose stood in the corner, throat hurting and head throbbing. The smell of lavender was unavoidable. She suspected there was still soap in her hair.

Someone sidled into the patch of old carpet next to

her. Rose could make out the braids in her peripheral. That and the very pregnant belly.

Blake might not have been a sheriff anymore, but her presence was no less intimidating. Thankfully, Rose had known Blake since they were kids, and that intimidation had never put her off the woman. She found it instead to be more of a comfort.

"Are we going to gloss over the fact that our dear Detective Williams seems to be closer to Brandy Lane than we originally thought or are we going to talk about it at length and with a lot of imagined details?"

Blake was smiling. She was trying to lighten the mood.

Rose appreciated it.

"You think there's something there just because our stern, closed-off, very blunt Darius suddenly has this trust in someone we've never even known he was on speaking terms with?" She snorted. "Of course we're going to talk about this. Just let me see if I can survive this Brandy Lane's kindness first and then I'm all in for gossip."

Blake stiffened next to her. The little lightness she had tried to bring in was gone. She lowered her voice even though James and Darius were in the bathroom.

"This time, we made sure that only a handful of us know you two are staying here. In fact, only a few of us even know about what happened right now. Liam and Price are dealing with that man with a firm grip. We're keeping a lid on the whole attack as much as possible." She thumbed over her shoulder to the motel room's door. "We have different cars now, we all made sure no one followed us from James's house, and all communication between you and us have gone to personal phones and computers."

"You think someone at the department leaked that I was staying at James's instead of my apartment? Even after we tried to be careful about it?"

It had been a question dogging all of them already—how anyone could even know she was at James's house in the first place—but Rose had a hard time believing someone at the department had been the one to spill the beans. At least, not on purpose. A sentiment Blake seemed to agree with.

"Not intentionally, but we can't ignore the fact that we're all human and live in a small, usually boring, town. If even one person mentioned it to their friends or family, that would be all it took to get the town's gossip mill up and turning. So this time, we're locking the knowledge up as tightly as possible." Blake, who had switched out with her husband at James's house once it was time to leave, looked thoughtful for the first time since then. "What about James, though?" she continued. "Do we need to worry about him talking to anyone? Anyone close to him?"

"He's single."

The words popped out of Rose's mouth before she could stop them.

Blake cast her a sidelong glance. It burned Rose to see that the woman also seemed to be clamping down on a smile.

"Oh, is he, now?" Blake lowered her voice even more. It sounded suspiciously mischievous. "Did our little Little gain that knowledge naturally or did she go fishing for it?"

If Blake hadn't been pregnant—and honestly, so much taller than Rose—she would have shoulder-checked her. As it was, she gave Blake a hefty eye roll.

"It came up in a conversation about our lives while we were hiding out. You know, from people trying to kill me."

Blake met her with an answering eye roll.

"Don't you try and guilt me just because I'm asking a reasonable personal question," she said. "Darius isn't the only one acting out of pocket."

As if on cue, James exited the bathroom in deep conversation with the detective.

Blake didn't point to him or nod his way, but Rose knew they were both all eyes on the man.

"You don't seem to mind him sticking to you."

Rose didn't know what to say to that—mostly because it was true—and was instead saved by the man himself. He walked over to them and put his hands on his hips, his brow knitted together in what felt like a subordinate giving a slightly off-putting report to a superior.

With them, though, it turned into James dropping his chin so he could stare down into the much smaller Rose.

"Despite no one using it for a bit, this place is pretty good, other than needing a bit of quick dusting," he started. "It was good on Brandy Lane to keep the power and water running too, or else this wouldn't be ideal. I'm going to start cleaning and get these sheets and blankets switched out while y'all finish up your conversation." He looked to Blake. "Unless there's something else you need from me?"

Darius and Blake answered in unison that there wasn't.

The two men went to get the supplies James had thought to bring from his house out of the car while Blake tapped the suitcase she had rolled into the room earlier.

"With the help of our FBI agent friend, we got you some more things from your apartment. Clothes, toiletries and some snacks he found in the pantry he thought you might like."

Rose's eyes widened. Blake read her thoughts.

"Don't worry. I've known the agent for a long time. He was respectful with it and even had his wife on the phone while he packed to make sure he got what you might need." Blake rubbed a hand over her stomach. "I would have done it myself, but it was decided that was a risk not worth taking."

Just in case there was another attacker lying in wait for Rose.

She didn't spell that out, though, and Blake didn't either. Instead, they said their goodbyes after James finished bringing in the rest of their things.

Then, after one last warning to be safe, it was just Rose and James alone again. It was an odd feeling to watch him. She had settled into one of the two worn wooden chairs by the air-conditioning unit and, like fireflies during a summer night, her attention seemed to flicker and float around him alone.

He hummed. She couldn't make out the tune, but it was upbeat. Slow in some parts, fast in others. He bobbed his head to match the beat sometimes, but no matter what, he focused on the chore he was currently attending to without missing a step.

He dusted every surface in the room with careful dedication. The nightstands, the table next to her, the chest of drawers opposite the bed, and even the curtains. From there he wiped them down with cleaner spray and wipes before going into the bathroom to presumably do the same. He came back and set to the flannel bundle he'd brought in earlier. True to word, it was a new set of sheets, pillowcases and quilt top.

Rose watched in absolute awe while he redid the bed as if it was the most normal situation there was.

When he was done, he took both of their bags and situated them on top of the chest of drawers.

Then he placed his hands on his hips, did a slow turnaround to survey their space, and then, seemingly pleased with himself, nodded.

"This place isn't that bad now," he said. "Honestly, the paint job here is probably better than my place."

Rose wanted to smile, she really did, but it was like sitting down had drained whatever she had left fueling her everything-is-fine guise. It was disappointing to realize that she couldn't fake it anymore, especially after getting her gusto back once she had finished crying earlier.

James filled the silence after a moment.

"I'm going to test out the shower really quick." He went to double-check the locks on the door, the clamp, and peeked out of the window. He drew back and nodded, once again to himself. Rose was starting to like the habit. As if he was constantly in a conversation with himself, and winning.

"Here, come keep me company," he added.

Rose felt her eyes widen but he merely explained by picking up the other chair. He walked it over to the bathroom and set it down just inside of the doorway.

James came back for a change of clothes, a towel he had also had the mind to pack, and then he came for her.

"I know you're strong and fearless and can handle anything thrown your way, but what we went through tonight got to me, and I'd feel a whole lot more comfortable if we could stick together for the rest of it." He outstretched his free hand. "You don't have to do anything but sit and listen to me chatter."

If it had been anyone else, she would have laughed at how ridiculous the request was. Yet, Rose took his hand. A moment later, she was sitting in another old wooden chair, facing the bed, the rest of the bathroom behind her.

True to his word, he started up the chatter quickly.

Rose listened enough to know she wasn't needed for it. He talked about Mr. Donahue and another client. Then he was talking about his trip he'd taken once to the mountains.

Rose floated in and out of the conversation long enough to catch a few points.

He liked the mountains and snow.

He liked hiking too but preferred to bike.

There was a breakfast shop he'd been to and it was nice.

He liked breakfast, especially omelets.

He'd never made an omelet for anyone other than his parents before.

He thought it might rain in the next few days.

When the shower cut off, she wasn't sure if she had missed anything else. If she did, James didn't fault her for it.

He dressed in silence behind her. When he was done with that, he reached around and patted her shoulder. She turned and looked up, up and up at him.

Gold with green and brown, all dancing around together in his eyes.

He asked a question, and she nodded in answer.

It wasn't until she was bent over, her head against the lip of the sink, and warm water running in tandem with his fingers over her hair, that she realized what he had offered.

James Keller, the giant who had broken a man's nose like it was nothing, gently washed out the last of her earlier bath's soap from her hair. And when the job was done, he kept on going.

Without one word between them he brushed her hair out and patted it dry. A new change of clothes came next. They weren't hers but Rose couldn't find time to care. When that was done, the distance between the bathroom and the bed blurred. Warm hands led her along it and then she blinked, and that warmth had turned into a sea of flannel around her.

Somewhere, in the back of her mind, Rose knew she had finally broken down. Just as she knew that, during the entire conversation in the shower, she had been staring at the lone bed in their room.

She shouldn't be this close to James, a stranger. She shouldn't accept his help or pity. She shouldn't endanger him or the things he loved all for her mistake. She shouldn't have let him get close. She shouldn't let him get closer.

Yet, when the time finally came for the lights to go out, Rose couldn't be bothered to care when the space next to her in bed was filled with by a man she'd just met a little over a week ago.

Because there was one thing Rose knew to be true more than all the rest.

James was warm.

And, to her, that was enough.

Chapter Twelve

The window unit might have looked old, but it worked more than fine. James felt the coolness on his face and his arm that had found its way on top of the quilt. It was the first thought he had once he had woken. The second was, despite the obvious chill in the air, parts of his body beneath the sheets were unusually warm.

James opened his eyes and was met with the popcorn ceiling of the Seven Roads Motel staring back at him. The blackout curtains must have shifted during his cleaning the night before. A strip of sunlight ran from the window and into a bright line across the ceiling fan that had wobbled too much to be used.

He knew why he was waking up to this and not his room at the house.

He remembered what had happened.

And yet the surprise of what was making him so warm still got him.

James peered down at his chest and saw the reason why he had woken up warm.

Rose was on her side but also on *his* side. She had one arm thrown over his chest while the corresponding leg was intertwined with his. Her head was resting on top of the hollow of his shoulder, a position made easier to achieve thanks to his own accommodation. James realized his arm was around her, holding her securely against his side.

Had going to sleep in the same bed last night been an issue in his mind? No, simply because he had only been worried about the blank look tugging Rose's expression down.

He had wanted to make her feel safe, was all. Secure, despite the madness that had been surrounding them.

Maybe he should have worried more, offered to sleep on the floor or one of the chairs. Given her space.

But James hadn't wanted to be apart from her.

He'd wanted to be close, just within reach if she needed him.

Though he hadn't thought about it quite like this.

James didn't know what to rightly do as he stared down at Rose's sleeping face. She had already become oddly endearing to him over the last week or so—someone he wanted to help protect and get justice for—but there had also been another feeling growing alongside his protectiveness.

Appreciation.

James couldn't help but mentally applaud so many things about the wildcard. Her smarts, her tenacity, her drive for helping others. But there was another thing he had been overlooking too.

Rose Little wasn't just cute, she was beautiful.

Asleep, awake, mad or angry. Smiling or annoyed. Sitting in a hospital bed, standing calm next to a bomb, or lying fast asleep against him.

Rose was a sight and a half and James couldn't help

but feel like he had slighted himself by not becoming her friend earlier.

Friend.

Was that what she was to him? Simply a friend?

James was about to try and pin down exactly what he might feel for the deputy when, among the list of things she was, he realized asleep wasn't one of them anymore.

Rose stretched her arm out over him like a cat might do after waking from a nap. Her leg followed suit before she started to nuzzle her face against his shoulder.

James was almost certain she hadn't yet realized what she was holding wasn't a pillow or blankets and decided to wait her out.

He didn't have to wait long.

Rose's body tensed comically fast.

James couldn't help it, he laughed.

"I think I might call you Little Furnace from now on," he rumbled out. "You generate a surprising amount of heat."

Maybe it wasn't the right thing to say. Maybe he should have been more considerate of the situation even though he wasn't sure what that situation was. Had Rose gotten close to him during the night on purpose or was she just the kind of person who cuddled up to whoever and whatever she was next to?

And if she had done it on purpose, had it been because she needed any sense of comfort, or had he been the specific one she needed comfort from?

James could have spiraled down a rabbit hole of questions—not even touching the subseries of the ones surrounding his own feelings on the matter—but Rose cut him off with a surprising twist of events.

She rocketed up but didn't move away from him. Instead, she whirled around and looked down at him with wide eyes and a barely contained smile.

Rose went from lying comfortably against him to tearing herself out of the bed like he had bitten her. She tucked and rolled off the edge so fast that James sat up quick to try and see if he needed to help her.

The sudden movement made his head throb. He winced at the pain.

Rose, managing to get to her feet, saw it.

He watched her face go from red to concerned and red. Her brows knitted together, her hands still clutching some of the quilt.

"Why are you doing that? What hurts?" she asked.

James touched his forehead.

"The part of my head I used as a battering ram yesterday." It was definitely sore. Probably bruising. "It's not a big deal, though. Just a little uncomfortable."

Rose didn't seem to believe him. She crawled back into bed and right over to him. Her eyes were locked on to the spot in question as she got almost close enough to touch it. James kept his mouth shut while she did her silent inspection.

When she was apparently okay with what she was seeing, she pulled back to sitting on her side of the bed and James saw her own set of bruising. It wasn't as pronounced as he would have thought it would be, but the once-handprint ring around her neck was still visible.

James tapped his own neck.

"How about that?" he asked. "How's that on the pain scale?"

Rose tentatively felt the area. She didn't wince.

"Fine as long as I don't touch it."

"How about your throat? You don't sound as raspy as you did last night."

Rose thought about it a moment.

"It's better," was all she came up with.

"Good."

James gave Rose some space to collect her own thoughts and stretched out wide before scooping up his phone. Rose excused herself to the bathroom. The shower turned on soon after. James couldn't help but give another little laugh.

Usually when he woke up with a woman, they would talk about what had happened or at least make a comment or two. Rose, though, wasn't like other women, he was finding.

No one had called or texted James since his last communication with his dad the night before. Still, he decided to send a few quick texts to his parents. They were simple messages, just saying good morning and to have a good day, but it was small interactions like those that meant a lot to James. Especially when his mother replied with a little picture of a kitten half-asleep next to an oversize mug.

That was why he was smiling when Rose reappeared, wrapped in a towel and hair dripping wet. Adrenaline shot through James as he was sure something was wrong, but this time her expression halted any action.

"I think I get it," she said in a flurry of barely contained excitement.

"Get what?"

"Why Damon has been attacking me like he has, instead of just outright killing me easy."

James didn't like the way she phrased it but he was also invested.

A smirk pulled up the corner of her lips.

James was once again bowled over by how beautiful the woman was.

"I think it's time we paid our friend from last night a visit."

AN HOUR LATER, Rose was standing between the bed she had slept in, the man she had slept with in it, and the sheriff of Seven Roads. It was a triangle she hadn't thought she'd ever be a part of but there she was, not only in it but excited to be there.

Simply because she had finally found a piece to the bizarre puzzle to finally make the last week less bizarre.

Price, settled in the corner, looking half-dead as he clung to his coffee cup, was the opposite of enthused. According to a quick chat with Liam he was ending a shift of helping Darius. When he had heard Rose wanted to talk about a possible lead, he had decided to end his night with the news.

Looking at him now, she wondered how bad *she* must have looked the night before. Just thinking about it was nothing compared to how she had woken up. She had been more attached to James than a koala to a tree.

What was worse?

James hadn't at all seemed fazed.

In fact, he had joked.

The situation would have been more mortifying if her shower hadn't dislodged a memory. One that she was more than excited to share now.

"The big thing that has been bothering me so much

about everything that has happened in the last week is how absolutely unnecessary Damon's attacks have been," she started, once all their attention was back on her. "A bomb in and of itself is a big, big thing and usually fits a particular pattern or has some kind of reason behind it. With Damon, though? He has no history of being remotely involved in explosions or using them to act out his anger. And you said that the bomb maker even confirmed he was hired for this one bomb?"

She asked the question to Price, but the sheriff answered for him.

"Yeah, the maker said he accepts small jobs and the FBI agent working the case had a file full of two jobs he'd done before for clients. All he had on Damon was a one-time meeting and two messages found from a burner phone."

Rose nodded.

"Then there's the gunmen who showed up at the garage," she went on. "Four of them hired completely separate from the bomb maker but with the job to follow my car."

"And, according to their snitch, they were supposed to watch you and only act if something happened to your car," Liam added. "Then, when they did act, they were told to shoot to kill."

Rose snapped her fingers.

"Which makes no sense," she jumped in. "It's like Damon wants to kill me but make it unnecessarily difficult for himself. Then there was the man last night."

A shiver tried to run itself down Rose's back. She suppressed it but knew James was watching her do it.

As she spoke he moved to her side to lean against the chest of drawers she was standing in front of.

"Darius said you found out who he is, right?"

It was Price who nodded now.

"Duncan Danvers," he said. "Last known to live an hour from here and on probation for assault and battery. He's not…the brightest of the bunch but he also refused to say a word until a lawyer got to him."

"And as far as we know, none of the gunmen, the bomb maker, or Danvers are connected," Liam said. "Other than the gunmen and the bomb maker being contacted by Damon at one point."

Rose hadn't recognized the attacker in James's house or his name. Which helped make her point even more.

"So, let's just say for argument's sake that this Duncan guy was also hired by Damon to take me out… He could have done it several times over if he'd simply brought a weapon." Out of her peripheral vision Rose saw James tense. She knew he still felt guilty for her being attacked in his home, but it wasn't his fault. None of this was. "Instead, this Duncan guy specifically said he had never drowned someone before, like he had waited patiently for me to get into the bathroom before coming in. Doesn't all of this sound ridiculous?"

The men around her agreed.

"Some people *are* ridiculous," Price offered. "Maybe Damon likes being flashy in his supposed acts of revenge. It's not like we haven't run into other dramatic perps who did a whole lot when doing a little would have gotten the job done."

"And normally I would agree but this morning I remembered a conversation I had about the video of me going viral after the bus situation." Rose pictured the reporter at the hospital, cast on his arm and anger in his gaze. "He said I was acting like some kind of action hero…because that's what some people called me. An action hero."

Rose handed her phone over to Liam. She had an article already up on the screen.

"More specifically this one article that went viral along with the video of me."

Liam started to read the article without being asked to. When he got to the part she wanted him to see, his eyes widened.

"Okay, stop leaving me in suspense," Price said from the corner. "Don't leave me hanging. What does it say?"

Rose opened her mouth to respond but Liam was faster. His tone had a new, undeniable hint of excitement.

Not happiness at what was happening but at the idea of having a new lead.

"The article talks about her bravery and breaks down what it means to be an action hero. He goes over his favorite stereotypical problems that the heroes go through during their time in the spotlight. There's… There's a list."

Price was done with sitting. He hurried over and shared in reading.

Rose didn't need to see it again. After remembering hearing about the article, she'd pulled it up with a quick Google search. She and James had read it several times while waiting for Liam and Price to show up.

James proved how well he had been paying attention

too, as he recalled the three situations that had more than caught their eye when reading it earlier.

"The classic group of lackeys that eventually turn on each other. The bomb strapped to someone the hero loves. And then—"

"'—the drowning scene, bonus points for the hero being trapped in some kind of vehicle while it's happening,'" Price finished, reading directly from the post.

Whether the coffee had finally hit his system, or the article had, his eyes were wide-open now.

"We don't have a body of water near here large enough for that, but I imagine a bathtub will do in a pinch," Rose said.

Liam shook his head. Price mimicked it.

"So, what are we guessing here?" he asked. "That Damon is pretending you're in some kind of movie where you're the lead?"

Rose didn't have any solid proof—she didn't even know much about the man himself—but as soon as she had read the article, she felt it to be true.

It was a theory but a theory that made sense.

"Because of that viral video, for one moment in time I was praised around the world for being a hero," Rose said, finally getting to the bottom line. "And I think, now the brother of the one person I didn't save wants me to die like one too."

Chapter Thirteen

Liam and Price took off with promises that they, along with Darius, would figure everything out. Rose stood by the window, peeking around the curtain like a little kid watching her parents run off to have fun without her.

She turned around, clearly dejected.

It was another endearing moment for the woman.

James doubted she was in the mood for the compliment.

"You said you trust them, and they do good work," he reminded her without preamble. "So we should let them go and do that good work."

Rose heaved out a long sigh.

"I did say that, and I do trust them, but I want to *help* them too," she wallowed. "This whole thing is about me, after all. Just sitting around here with you isn't doing anything but wasting time."

James made a pained sound and clutched at his chest.

"Wow, Wildcard. Way to hit me where it hurts."

Rose openly scanned his expression. She must have judged his words as the joke he intended. She waved through the air between them with slight annoyance.

"You know I don't mean being with you is a waste,"

she corrected. “I mean us sitting here with nothing to do is a waste.”

Another moment of endearment.

He smiled into it.

Rose was too distracted to note it. Her brow was crinkled, and her gaze seemed to hollow. Those gears that never seemed to stop turning were going faster again.

“There’s got to be something we can do… Let’s talk it out one more time? It just all feels so ridiculous that I’m having a hard time processing alone in my head.”

James waved his hand.

“Then join me out here and I’ll help the best I can.”

Rose nodded and started to pace across the seen-better-days carpet. Her hair was cinched up tight in a slick bun that contrasted with the casual cut of her clothes. The boots she had put on gave her an inch of height but she still looked impossibly small making a groove in the carpet as she went back and forth. If he had seen her without context, he couldn’t have imagined anyone would go to such lengths to hurt her.

Though, maybe he was projecting his own surprising yet steady feelings of protectiveness for the woman.

“The author of that article is, according to the website, based in Mississippi,” she started. “If Darius doesn’t find anything that links him to Damon, I’m going to assume Damon found the article and is just using it as his own plan.”

“It *was* one of the most viewed press pieces during that time,” James said. “Even the comments on it had a lot of interaction.”

She nodded. Then she paused.

"So let's say that's his outline as a middle finger up to everyone calling me an action hero. But why wait five months to do any of it? Was it a funding thing? Was it a planning thing? Why wait that long?"

James hadn't thought about that yet.

The timing of it was a little odd.

"Maybe it was a grief thing?" he offered. "Or, you know, he might not have instantly wanted his revenge against you. Something could have triggered him sometime after." He didn't know how true that was, though. Darius had confirmed with the bomb maker that he had been hired by Damon less than a month after the bus incident. "Or the gap could be because he was getting Derrick's affairs in order. Didn't you say their parents were much older and lived up North?"

"Yeah, but I'm not sure how hands-on Damon might or might not have been." Rose's voice went soft. "To be honest, I don't really know much about Damon. I only spoke to him once. At the hospital. After he identified Derrick's body. It wasn't a very pleasant conversation on any front."

James had wanted to ask about this before, because, aside from him doing an internet search, he also didn't know much about the man behind the attacks. Only what Rose had told him at the sheriff's department, a conversation that felt like it had happened years ago and not a day. Now, though, any and all details could be important, so he didn't hold back with his questions anymore.

"How *did* that conversation go? Between you and Damon, I mean."

Rose slowed her pacing.

"I shouldn't have talked to him but I—I was upset. Guilt and anger and being so dang tired from all that adrenaline finally leaving my system. I *shouldn't* have talked to him, but I did." She sighed. "I apologized for hesitating and that opened a can of really angry worms. He had me detail out everything that happened and I told him everything I told you."

"The fight between that Lloyd guy and Derrick on the bus, you mean?"

She nodded.

"Poor Lloyd too, he just happened to walk by when I was done. Derrick went over to him and, even though I couldn't hear what they were saying, they were definitely heated. Price eventually had to break their fight up and send—"

Rose came to a halt.

"Lloyd," she said, interrupting herself.

"Lloyd?" James repeated.

Her dark eyes were like saucers when they swung to his.

"I understand targeting me after the viral video and press, but don't you think some of that anger might have gone to the man who actually fought Derrick?"

James didn't know why he hadn't given another thought to Lloyd before. Now a rising sense of urgency pulled at his gut.

"When is the last time you saw Lloyd? At the hospital after the storm?"

Rose took her phone off the small table. Her thumbs were lightning-fast across the screen. Still, she answered.

"I actually ran into him at the hospital about a month

ago when I was visiting Doc Ernest… The Camden Pharmaceuticals people eat lunch in the hospital's cafeteria since the research annex doesn't have a big kitchen…" Her focus narrowed in on her phone.

James left her to her silence.

He hadn't known Rose all that long, but he thought he now had a handle on how she operated. At all times, Rose Little was charging forward, eager to protect someone. It made her brave and reckless and earned her the nickname Wildcard. She disregarded herself for the sake of others. It was mostly a commendable trait.

It was also a terrifying one for the people who cared about her.

And James cared.

He had since she had pulled him into the service pit, when she had agreed to pretend to be hurt at the sheriff's department to make him feel better, after he stood with her in the field behind his house, every second he had spent saving her from the tub the night before, and hours after he had shared a bed with her.

James cared about Rose to the point of distraction.

Something he hadn't felt in a very long time.

It was and wasn't surprising.

Rose Little may have been small, but she had more than proven she was absolutely mighty.

And he simply wanted more.

It was a quick epiphany. One that had James nod to himself to confirm he felt the change. Now wasn't the time to talk about it, though. Instead he kept to his chair and waited for the woman of the hour to plan her next move. Because no matter what it was, James knew he would follow.

She could protect everyone else, because James would protect Rose.

He just didn't realize then how quickly he was going to have to do so.

"Betrayed by someone you trust, a close-corridors fight in a precarious place, something to do with heights, and a high-speed car chase through a bustling city."

Rose was paraphrasing the last of Payton Abbot's favorite action hero encounters with as little enthusiasm as possible. She looked up at the giant wall of a man standing pressed up against an actual wall and narrowed her eyes.

"Unless you and the department have other plans, I don't think I'm going to get betrayed by someone I trust," she continued. "As for the close combat fight in a 'precarious' place—I'm not even sure what that means—and something to do with me being on the edge of a cliff or something, I feel like those could be difficult to mastermind even if Damon outsourced. I'm not even sure we can count the car chase one since we're not exactly a bustling city. But maybe the city part doesn't count. Damon seemed okay with changing the whole drowning thing to some random man ruining my bath."

James had had his eye on the doors to the hospital cafeteria for almost fifteen minutes. Even as he spoke now, he kept his gaze fixed.

"I'm not sure if you're talking about all of this like it's nothing as a way to cope or not, but let it be known, I'm not a fan of how casual you're making this sound."

Rose had already picked up on that fact. The man might have a calm poker face but his body always gave him away. He had been tense ever since they had come to the hospital, doubly so when Rose was recognized by one of her friends on the staff. Now she could see the tension clearly in the line of his shoulders and the tightness of his jaw.

That tightness managed to stay there when he added another thought, just as grumbly as the previous one.

"And let it also be known, that no, I will not be the one who betrays you. So you can throw that idea right on out."

Rose didn't say it, but she hadn't even entertained the idea of James betraying her in any sense of the word. An odd thing, considering she hadn't even known the sound of his voice until a week ago. Now that sound was a comfort. A promise of being there. A calm place in an extremely unorthodox storm.

Also a voice of reason.

Because James was right.

Joking about everything—being so casual talking about how determined someone was to take her life, money and prison time be damned—was the only thing keeping the panic in her down. She had already been stressed with the bomb and the gunmen at the garage but after the man in the bathroom?

Everything had changed.

Church clothes or not, that man had truly scared her by invading a space she'd never imagined would be dangerous. He had overpowered her quickly and had nearly taken her life. All while she had been naked.

That small detail might not have seemed like a big deal in the grand scheme of things, but to Rose, it might have been the worst part.

She had been utterly vulnerable, not a stitch on or no weapon in sight.

If it hadn't been for James…

Rose peeked up at the man again.

She didn't want to even think about it.

As if she had voiced her thoughts out loud, the man in question swung his golden-rimmed gaze her way. He thumbed back over his shoulder.

"Isn't that our guy?"

Adrenaline shot through her, breaking up thoughts of panic and of James and the comfort he brought. Rose swung her head around James's shoulder so fast that if she had been wearing her hair in a ponytail it would have smacked him good.

"That's definitely Lloyd," she confirmed, staring at the group of people who had just left the cafeteria. "Doc Ernest said the Camden people always take lunch at the same time during the week. He's the one in the back on his phone. The good-looking guy with the blond hair."

James snorted but was already moving. She heard him mutter beneath his breath.

"I didn't need that last part."

Rose didn't respond to his cheekiness. Instead, she let James take the lead and approach the group by himself. She held back out of sight. Only a few of the people who had been there during the storm still worked at Camden now. That didn't mean she wanted to chance falling into a catch-up by running into them. Her current plan was simple: see if Lloyd had had any contact with Damon since the storm or had any dangerous run-ins recently.

Rose didn't need to chat past that.

Lloyd seemed just as uninterested in the usual pleasantries when he rounded the corner with James in tow. His eyes widened at the sight of her, but he didn't smile.

"Deputy Little, what a coincidence, I was just about to try and find you."

Rose shared a look with James.

Unlike the last time she had seen him, Lloyd Harrison looked somehow worse for the wear. Which was saying a lot, given their last danger-filled interaction had been in the middle of a flood and a tornado. There were dark circles beneath eyes that were tinged red. He also seemed to have lost some weight.

Maybe Rose wasn't the only one Damon had been targeting after all.

"You were looking for me?" she asked.

Lloyd nodded. His tired gaze shifted between her and James before he lowered his voice.

"I think it's time we had a talk." He nodded to James but kept his eyes on her. "A very private one."

Chapter Fourteen

James had no idea what was going on, but he did know everything had gone wrong.

"Rose!" he yelled, not for the first time.

The woman might have been small in size but what she lacked in height she more than gained in speed. She ran full tilt down the hospital hallway like she was running for her life. The problem with that?

James was the only one behind her.

"Sto-stop!" he yelled out, nearly tripping over a patient coming out of a room. He sidestepped the confused woman and focused back on running after the woman confusing him.

Rose started to slow but only so she could take a turn in the hallway. He could hear her shoes squeak across the floor. James wanted to use her slower pace to his advantage, but it just wasn't in the cards, with his physique. He took the turn a lot less gracefully than her, losing him even more distance between them.

What had happened?

Why was she running?

James chanced the quickest of looks back down the hallway he was leaving.

There was no one chasing them. Absolutely no one.

But it had to have something to do with that Lloyd guy. If he had time, James would have cursed the man. He never should have stepped aside to give Lloyd the privacy to talk to Rose.

"Listen, he obviously looks scared," Rose had argued when it was clear James didn't want her to be alone with the man. "He could have some answers. Some answers we need. And he could also need *us*. If Damon blames me for not saving Derrick because of a hesitation and he's been going through all of this? Maybe he's been doing much worse to someone else."

Rose had reached out and put her hand right into James's. It was small and warm and soft. Her expression was none of those. Her expression was hard, sharp. Determined, angry. Excited for something. Ready for anything.

Wildcard Rose.

She wasn't asking permission.

Not that he would have been in the right to give it.

So he had relented, but only so much.

"I'll go stand over there so I can keep you in my sight," he had warned. "No going into off-limits rooms or secret passageways to make Damon's job easier for him."

She had nodded and pointed out a spot at the intersection of the hallway he had been standing in.

"Out in the open but not in a crowded place *and* you can see me."

That had been fine. That had been good.

That still hadn't worked.

Rose and Lloyd had started talking without any issue. Lloyd seemed tired, Rose open to listening to whatever he was saying. No one passed through their hallway or James's. No gunmen or Damon or creep in a collared shirt showed.

And then everything had changed.

Rose hadn't even looked his way before she turned on her heel and ran out of sight. Lloyd did the same.

But in the opposite direction.

By the time James had made it to their hallway, the choice of whom to follow had been a no-brainer.

Now that no-brainer had him thoroughly confused.

Rose wasn't stopping for him.

Why?

The hallway they turned into wasn't as long as the one they had come from. If he was tracking right, it turned into the back section of the hospital before hitting a bank of elevators. There was a doctor's clinic somewhere near here that he had taken Mr. Donahue to once. A clinic in the hospital that had its own small parking lot.

Where they had parked earlier before walking around the other side of the hospital to avoid as many eyes as possible.

That Rose, he realized, was heading straight for.

He heard the impact of her throwing open the Exit doors to the parking lot before he saw daylight streaming through them.

"Rose! Stop!"

She didn't.

The doors shut before James could reach them. When it was his turn to open them, it sounded like an explosion as he rammed right on through.

Heat hit him in the face and made the sweat already

starting to bead down him gain more traction. James didn't care. He wasn't going to stop running until he caught her. Even if that meant running every inch of the hospital or—

James felt his stomach sink.

He had driven to the hospital in the truck they had borrowed from a deputy at the department…but Rose had the keys. She had taken them after he had complained that the key ring was too bulky for his jeans.

Now he wished more than anything he hadn't been such a baby about it.

Just then he saw what Rose's speed had won her.

Halfway across the lot, she was already getting inside the truck. James didn't bother calling for her again. Whatever was happening, she didn't want him to be a part of it.

But that didn't stop him from trying.

James pushed his big muscles as far as they would go at the truck with all he had.

Wildcard Rose?

Not even a man like him could catch her if she didn't want him to.

She slammed on the gas as soon as the truck started.

James missed her by mere seconds.

Rose not once looked his way.

Wherever she was going, she was going to face it alone.

ROSE WASN'T USED to the truck. She didn't know how much speed it could handle and how much grace she needed to give it without letting her foot off the gas pedal. Instead of playing it completely safe, but also not putting her entire life on the line by slinging it around at ninety miles an hour, she split the difference.

When she came to the metal gate that separated the Reynolds Farm and the Seven Roads Cemetery right off County Road 72's start, she hit it at a cool forty miles an hour.

The truck whined at the hit, bumped her around a little, metal twisted a little more, but it took out the gate without taking her out. And it didn't pop a tire as far as she could tell.

Small blessings, she thought, as she started to haul tail again.

The Seven Roads Cemetery had changed names three times in its one-hundred-year existence. No one really got buried there anymore and not many people in town had people already there, so the through traffic had become less and less over the last few years. Five months ago, the entire place had been shut down after the storm dislodged some graves and nearly destroyed the main office.

Damage or not, though, Rose knew her way around.

Knuckles white against the steering wheel, she bypassed the decapitated office and took the main road that ran around the entire two-acre plot of land. Gravestones, old and weathered, dotted the land to her right. Big oaks, some damaged from the same storm, were lined up at her left. Her target, though, would be right up ahead in a few seconds.

Rose's stomach tightened as the phone in her pocket vibrated.

She knew who it would be.

She knew what he would say if she answered.

She knew what he would say when she told him why she was out here.

James would tell her to turn around. To stop. To wait.

To not listen to Lloyd's warning.

To not willingly go into danger.

To not make it easier for Damon…

But what James didn't realize was that she was doing this for him.

"While you've been dodging his attacks, I've been playing his games," Lloyd had said, exhaustion in his every word.

"Damon's?" she had parroted.

Lloyd had sighed.

"He sure started it," he'd said. "I thought I found a way out but then you finally showed up."

"I don't understand. What game? What's going on?"

There had been no hesitation in Lloyd's answer, no emotion either. Just that exhaustion. How had his co-workers not seen it? How had no one stopped him to check on him?

"I've been playing hide-and-seek," he'd said, not at all showing signs that he was kidding. "But only one person can find me and you just did." He'd glanced down at his phone. "And he knew you were here before I did. He sure is everywhere."

Lloyd had sighed again, an all-consuming weight seemingly dragging him down. Rose had almost turned to James then, red flags springing up to make a sea around them, but Lloyd had been quick.

"Don't let him know what I'm about to tell you or we're both going to lose."

Lloyd had just finished a phone call when they had first seen him, and he let her in on the conversation.

"We have ten minutes to get to the groundskeeper's house at the Seven Roads Cemetery. If we're not there by then and if we're not alone, bad things will happen to whoever they took."

Rose hadn't for the life of her expected that.

"Whoever they took?"

Lloyd had flinched.

"That's all he said."

The sea of red flags took over the land too.

Lloyd, however, hadn't tried to reassure her or persuade her after that. But she wasn't sure any words could convince her faster than his utter look of resignation.

Rose had believed Lloyd then.

Still, she wasn't a fool.

"We could still call for help," she'd said.

Lloyd had shaken his head.

"I'm not taking that chance again. I've already learned my lesson." He had flinched again before putting his phone in his pocket. "The time starts when we leave the hospital. What do you want to do about the big guy over there? He looks like he'll stop us and get himself killed for it."

Every word Lloyd had said lacked inflection, lacked emotion. Just matter-of-fact.

It sealed the deal for Rose right then and there to take this seriously.

There had been too many unknowns.

What she *had* known was she wasn't going to lead

James into a situation that would put him and someone else in danger.

"My car is in the side lot," she had said.

Lloyd, despite his obviously deteriorated emotional state, had understood.

"We'll split up," he'd said. "Whatever happens, I suggest you get there in ten minutes."

Rose had wanted to turn to James, to call his name, to take him with her, but she put her trust into fear.

Now she had two minutes left as the side road that branched off to the house behind the cemetery came into view.

Everyone local to Seven Roads knew about Groundskeeper Demetri's old house. Demetri was the last person to live there and die there, and since his time it had become the famed haunted house of the town. Teens went there on haunt nights and spoke to Old Demetri like he was a ghost lying in wait just for them. It was an easy way to kill boredom on a Friday night and an easier excuse to snuggle up with a special someone when things got too spooky.

Rose couldn't fault anyone for it because she had been part of some of the first groups of teens to start the tradition of haunt nights and fake ghost-whispering. Blake and Price had even shown up a time or two with her, because when you grew up in a place as boring as Seven Roads, you had to get creative.

Now, seeing the old two-story, Rose felt true fear grip at her heart.

Not only because of the unknown but because there had been a detail about the property she had forgotten.

There was a small pond behind the abandoned house.

Was that why she had been told to come there? For another attempt at a drowning scene?

Or was this just part of Damon's revenge for Lloyd?

Rose shook her head to herself and slammed on brakes, skidding to a stop on the overgrown grass next to the house. Her phone started to vibrate again.

She ignored it.

If she was wrong, it was only her life in danger.

If she was right and coming could save someone? Could keep James safe?

Those odds she could make peace with.

Rose didn't waste any more time. She ran up to the porch and took the steps two at a time. She went for the door handle, but the door was already cracked open. She pushed it open with her foot and on reflex went for her gun.

It wasn't there.

Neither was anyone in the foyer.

Rose listened but heard nothing but her heartbeat thundering in her chest.

Was this part of the movie scene? Was this part of a game? *Had* Lloyd told this bizarre lie simply to separate her from James?

No sooner did she start to doubt everything than she finally heard something in the distance. She walked in its direction, going from the old foyer to the kitchen that was at the back of the house. In its prime, it was probably the most beautiful of rooms with big, open windows running along almost every wall, facing out toward the dock and pond. Great for watching sunrises and sunsets and making the job of groundskeeper all the more relaxing.

Now some of the windows had long since been broken. Others had molded. Some had vines that had come through. One had plastic poorly taped across it.

Yet, despite the dilapidated state of them, Rose could see what she realized was just for her.

She also understood the noise she was hearing.

A man was standing on the dock, clapping. There was something next to him but she couldn't make it out completely.

Not that it mattered much.

Something had been set in motion, and it was time for her to find out what and why.

So she took a quick breath and pushed open the back door. Once upon a time it had led to a patio that had housed many a party back in her day. House bands and wannabe DJs, kegs and constant chatter. She'd had fun here then. Dancing, talking, playing around. A teenager without too much to worry about, thinking only about how to kill boredom.

Twenty or so years later, Rose walked across the same concrete with a heaviness that only grew with each new step.

Because the man clapping was none other than Damon Tillman.

And now she could clearly see what he was standing next to.

It was two cinder blocks. If that wasn't terrifying enough, the rope hanging around his arm sure did the trick.

Chapter Fifteen

No one had yet asked *why* Rose hesitated to reach out to Derrick Tillman. She suspected that the few who knew she felt responsible for his death thought she did so because the situation had been chaotic. There was a tornado coming, a flood already raging, and eleven ducks she had been tasked with single-handedly getting in a row.

It had been a lot, so hesitating might have just been a problem with the environment.

But that wasn't true.

Rose had hesitated for the same reason her feet faltered as she walked out onto the dock now.

When she had reached out to Derrick on that bus, she had seen something so intense that her body had reacted by simply stopping.

She had seen his expression.

More aptly, his rage.

It hadn't fit his face, contorting the youthful handsomeness into an awful mask of anger, making every angle across it a startling addition to the already nerve-wracking situation. In that moment, that anger had felt dangerous. Too dangerous, like a hammer racing toward a window that already had several cracks spiderwebbing across it.

So Rose had hesitated in caution.

Because every part of her at that time had believed that Derrick Tillman was ready to unleash that rage. And bringing him closer to the ten other ducks she needed to get to the pond?

Her body had acted before she could stop it.

We can't afford that anger, it had said.

She had squashed that thought a few seconds later, reminding herself that, anger or not, rage or not, he was still one of her ducks, but it had been too late.

Now, coming to a stop a few feet from Damon, she could see the same rage that his little brother had been wearing, written clearly across his face.

It didn't occur to her until that very moment to wonder where Derrick's anger had come from.

The origin of Damon's anger, however, was no secret.

"You know, I had no doubt you'd come here, Deputy."

His head was shaved close; dark hair matching an outfit that had been picked with stealth in mind. He wore black clothing and work boots. There was a cell phone in his left hand, a gun in his right.

He held the cell phone up to his sight line, but the gun was down at his side.

Rose glanced around the rest of the dock. There was more rope behind him, also another set of cinder blocks.

"The way I see it, I didn't have a choice," Rose said.

Damon laughed, though it was wholly unkind.

"Normally, I would have said you just like the attention, but now, I guess I understand it." His fake laughter melted. He was seething next. "This is why I've never liked them."

His phone vibrated and his gaze switched to its screen.

Whatever he saw must have been something he was waiting for. He nodded to himself.

Then he threw his phone into the water.

"Action heroes," he continued. His laughter came back. Again, there was no humor in it. "Did you know that Derrick was obsessed with them growing up? You couldn't walk into our house without seeing some kind of action movie on the TV. New ones, old ones, popular ones, ones that barely anyone had heard of…they were always there, filling the rooms of childhood." He smiled, briefly. "I asked Derrick once if he wanted to be one of the heroes he loved so much but he said no. He just liked the idea of them."

He sighed.

Rose looked at his finger next to the trigger.

"Someone, who by all accounts could have left the story at the beginning, decided to stay. To go against the insurmountable odds and try to make everything better."

The anger in him was still there but Rose didn't understand where he wanted it to go. Instead of being aimed at her, it seemed like it was burning him.

"Who did you take, Damon?" she ventured. "Where are they?"

Damon seemed surprised by the question. It smoothed into another smile that sent a shiver through her.

"Does it matter?" he asked. "It could be your parents or that boyfriend of yours or eleven strangers on a bus, you would always come, right? Because that's what heroes do."

A creeping cold started to move through Rose.

It was a lie.

Damon had no one.

No one but her.

And she had given herself over willingly.

Damon searched her expression. He nodded as if hearing her realization, but continued with his speech.

"But me? I never liked action movies. Those heroes Derrick loved so much? They were all the same. No matter the planning, the cause, the circumstances, they always found a way to fix everything. To come out on top. But we never saw all the choices that had to be made, all the consequences that had to happen. We never got to see everyone's problems and worries. Their burdens to bear. We didn't see the hospital bills, the cost of living, the price of milk."

He shook his head.

"We saw heroes escaping quicksand and badly trained men with guns. We saw car chases and fights in the subway. Bombs attached to toilets and bodies floating at the bottom of lakes."

Another shiver went down Rose's spine.

Damon didn't catch it.

He did, however, regard her with another pointed stare.

"You know, I think it was fate that they compared you to something Derrick—the man you didn't save—loved. I just wanted to show the world that you weren't a hero, after all. Not to Derrick, not to me."

Damon seemed more tired now than mad. His shoulders sagged a little.

Rose didn't understand the attitude.

He had her where he wanted, right?

No weapon, no backup. Just herself and good intentions.

"What do you want now, Damon? Why am I here?"

She eyed those cinder blocks.

Damon seemed unperturbed.

"Because the reason I dislike heroes the most is they're foolish," he said. "And I'm no fool."

He lowered his gun just as the sound of footfalls on the wooden dock behind her sounded.

Whoever the newcomer was, he didn't glance their way.

"Betrayal by someone you love was going to be my masterpiece at the end of all of this," he said. "But it looks like that's my scene now."

Damon threw his gun into the water like he had his phone.

Rose had no idea what was happening but, for some reason, she simply couldn't look away.

Because Damon Tillman was smiling again.

This time, there was no anger in it. No hate or rage.

This time, it seemed genuine.

His gaze moved over her shoulder.

He said one last thing before all hell broke loose.

It was simple.

"And I'm okay with it."

JAMES KNEW HE had only a short amount of time before the sheriff's department was on his tail. He didn't blame them or the man he had basically carjacked in the parking lot. Desperate times called for desperate measures and there was no way in hell he was going to just sit around while Rose had jetted off to who knew what. Much like during the chase through the hospital, Rose had a considerable lead ahead of him. It was only by sheer luck that he'd seen another car booking it out of the main lot by the time he reached the main road.

It was Lloyd Harrison.

Two cars managed to get between them before James could ride his tail and, because of those two cars, he was slowed down enough that he lost Lloyd on a turn onto County. James cussed up a storm as he raced down the new road without a car in sight.

There was no way Lloyd had been that fast. He had to have turned off somewhere.

No sooner had he had the thought than James spotted tire marks streaking through the dirt and grass off the shoulder ahead. He slowed.

Then he saw the metal gate of the Seven Roads Cemetery, on the ground, bent and broken.

Rose.

As soon as he was past the gate, he was more confident in his choice. Two sets of very distinct tire marks had kicked up dirt and grass along the road leading to the left. James followed that for what felt like an hour but must have really only been a minute or two. When the road started to curve to the right, though, he saw the trail of tire marks veer in the opposite direction. That road led in between trees, away from the open land of the cemetery plots.

James reduced his speed as he went left. If he had been a tried and true local, he would have probably known exactly where he was headed. Instead, he was caught off guard when a large house came into view in the distance.

It had seen better days, that was for sure.

It also had seen Rose.

Their borrowed truck was parked off to the side, alongside the vehicle Lloyd had been driving. James didn't even bother turning the car off. He barely put it in Park before he was leaping out and running.

The smell of mold and dust filled his nostrils. Humidity tightened its grip. James knew he wasn't, but it felt like he had been holding his breath since the hospital. There was no one and nothing that jumped out of him.

"Rose!" he yelled, caution now be damned.

Silence.

Was she somewhere in the house? Where and who else was here?

He ran to his left and into what must have been the old living area. She wasn't there. James ran in the other direction. His steps echoed.

"Rose!" he yelled again.

This time, the silence was gone.

"James!"

It was her. Faint, but he heard her.

He skidded to a stop before pivoting to go back to the entryway.

"Rose! Where are you?"

He heard her call him again. It was coming from outside.

James ran through a kitchen and through a door that was already wide-open. Two steps across the patio and he saw the dock. It was long, notably withered, and stood over a pond he'd never known existed.

If it had been a different situation, he might have appreciated the peaceful scenery.

But what he saw frightened him as much as it relieved him.

"Rose!"

At the end of the dock the most beautiful woman he had ever seen turned to her name.

He didn't know what he expected but when she yelled for him, he listened.

"Hurry!"

James ran so fast, at one point he wasn't even sure he was touching the ground. It was just pure propulsion from where Rose wasn't to the spot by her side. The closer James got, the more confusing the details became. No one was with Rose but there was blood on the wood next to her. The clothes she was wearing, however, were clean. The only thing that had changed since he had last seen her at the hospital was the rope she was currently untying from around her ankles.

Rope that was attached to a cinder block near the dock's edge. Two more cinder blocks were next to her.

She didn't seem like she was hurt. Yet her expression was panicked.

He didn't know why.

Rose pointed to the water.

"Save him," she yelled.

James didn't need to know more. He didn't need the details to make sense. Context wasn't the key to getting him to act.

It was Rose.

She needed him to do something.

So something was what he did.

Without a single question, James dove into the water.

The house might have been warm and the outdoor air humid, but the pond was absolutely cold. It hit James's body like a ton of bricks as he immediately started swimming downward. He opened his eyes once he adjusted and the cold was less jarring, and scanned the area.

He didn't know who this *he* was, and he didn't know why he needed saving, but the second James saw the body sinking toward the bottom, he readjusted his aim.

The man looked like he was standing straight up in the water, his arms suspended above his head, his shirt loose and floating in the same direction. James made it to his waist and realized how the cinder block fit into everything.

The man was tied to it.

Just like Rose was tied to one on the dock.

James didn't have time to be angry. The man wasn't moving.

He dove deeper down to try and see if the rope was tied around his ankles too. The water was murky, but James was able to find where the rope connected. Luckily it was around one ankle, not both.

Water displaced above him as James set to undoing the knot. He didn't turn to see who had jumped in. He knew it was Rose.

She attached to the other side of the man, using him to reorient herself so her feet were touching the ground. James's chest started to burn with the effort. He was running out of time.

Rose must have realized it too.

She reached out and touched him before pointing to the surface.

But James wasn't leaving her again.

Instead of dealing with untying the knot completely, James did the next best thing.

He ripped it apart.

Whether the knot was bad to start with or the rope was already frayed, it came undone fast. The man shifted and Rose's positioning finally made sense. She pushed off the ground with her arm wrapped around the man's waist.

Together with James, the three of them sprung up to the surface.

James hit it first, gulping up the air. Rose came second. She was already yelling for him.

"Help me! Help me get him to bank!"

It was a struggle at first but soon they found a system between them that worked. The man didn't fight back at all, which made sense considering he wasn't breathing when James hefted him up the bank and pulled him to a flat area of grass.

"He's—he's been in the water for—for over a minute," Rose huffed out. She shoved her hair off her face. She didn't meet his eye. "He's been—been shot too. I need—I need to call this in but my phone—"

James yanked his phone out of his pocket but felt instant relief.

"It's waterproof." He started a call to 9-1-1 while Rose put pressure on the bullet wound in question. It was near his shoulder and the sudden force didn't stir him either.

"Who is this?" he asked.

James was utterly shocked at her answer.

"It's Damon. I—I need you start CPR while I go—"

She tried to stand, James kept her down. He might not have known what had led to Damon being the one tied to a cinder block and shot, but he doubted it was Rose's doing, considering he had found her tied up too.

So there was a third person.

Someone he hadn't seen yet.

"Who shot him? Who tied you two up? Was it Lloyd?"

Her eyes widened. A dispatcher answered the call, her voice floating up toward them. Rose simply nodded.

"Where did he go?" James's muscles were tensing, his adrenaline surging one more time.

"The house. He's—he's armed."

James didn't give two licks.

He ran back to that house, clothes soaked through, and yelled Lloyd's name like an angry sermon.

What he hadn't counted on was the man calling him right on back.

Lloyd Harrison was standing by a window on the second floor. The window treatments were still there, framing the dirty glass with stubborn dignity. It was the only thing in that room that seemed to belong.

Lloyd didn't. In fact, he didn't look like he belonged anywhere. His clothes were baggy, his hair limp, his expression dull. He looked like he had already been written out of the world, but his body just hadn't caught up yet. He rested one hand on the window frame; the other was wrapped around a gun.

His gaze was slow as syrup as it moved between the outside world and James in the doorway.

James was dripping on the hardwood. His chest was heavy from anger and effort. His fists were empty but balled.

He had never met or seen Lloyd Harrison before that morning and now the man was squarely in his sights.

"You tied her to that block," he breathed out, his voice as low as he'd ever heard it himself.

Lloyd hardly reacted.

"Damon did," he said, voice just floating along. "Then I tied Damon up. Then I shot him and came here. I saw you two jump in to get him. I can see Rose is trying to save him now too. Because that's what heroes do."

James was taken aback at the honesty.

"You know, I don't much care for the whole hero thing or games, but I get now why Damon was so angry." A small, watery smile swirled over Lloyd's lips. "His brother used to call him a hero too, and then, the day he died was the day he stopped. I never really got how much that must have hurt until now."

He let out a breath. It was short and didn't drag him down. Instead, it seemed to be just another motion he was going through. Then he smiled again. James couldn't tell what emotion it was coming from, but it didn't feel fake.

"I don't think he ever really blamed Rose, though," he continued. "I know I don't. It wasn't her fault. It was…it was that storm. That damned generator." He let out a small laugh. "It's funny how one single point of failure can wreck so many things."

James took a tentative step forward. Why this man was waxing poetic, he didn't know, but that gun needed to be gone.

"I don't know what's going on, but it sounds like you shot a man who was aiming to hurt you and Rose. We can be calm and talk about the rest of it."

Lloyd didn't seem to mind him creeping closer.

James got the impression that Lloyd had stopped minding anything at all.

He let out one last little sigh.

"If you want this to end here, I suggest you don't repeat what I'm about to say, but, well, I think it should be said." He glanced out of the window. James was about to spring at him, but he raised the gun and placed it against his temple.

When Lloyd looked back at him, his smile was the only thing left that seemed alive.

"Damon is really good at tying knots, but Rose sure got out of it easy, didn't she? I could have pushed her in the water too, tied to that thing, but I didn't. I guess we're not all that bad, in the end." Lloyd turned back to the window. His last words haunted the empty room.

"Close your eyes now, Mr. Keller. This won't be pretty."

James ran forward, yelling.

He didn't make it.

The window treatments kept on hanging but Lloyd Harrison was gone.

Chapter Sixteen

Rose was screaming but she didn't move from her spot on that patch of grass.

"Shots fired!" she yelled down at the phone. "James? James!"

No one responded. The house was too far back, and she couldn't see which room the sound had come from.

She also couldn't stop.

She continued heart compressions on Damon Tillman while her own heart shattered around them both.

James had gone into the groundskeeper's house after Lloyd and now Lloyd had shot him, and Rose felt as helpless as a person could.

She could go see. She could leave Damon on the wet ground, covered in blood and not breathing, and no one would fault her for it. The man who had masterminded the attacks meant to kill her over the last week… The man who had told all his hired helpers that he was out for revenge. That for him to be happy, Rose had to die.

She could leave him right there.

And no one, *no one*, could say she did wrong.

Except…her.

Tears hot and heavy blurred her vision and streamed down her face. Her head hurt. Her heart hurt. The world hurt.

But she kept on with her compressions.

She wouldn't leave Damon Tillman any more than she would leave James had he been beneath her hands. Not when she could still help. Not when there was still hope.

But James could be the one who needs you now, up there, Rose couldn't help but think. *And you're here with someone who hated you so much.*

Rose didn't hesitate, despite herself.

In fact, a part of her believed that James would tell her to do the same.

Still, it hurt.

Rose screamed out in anger and fear and anguish and exhaustion.

She called James's name again, absolutely certain that Lloyd had used one shot to end him. A shot that he never would have taken had Rose stayed with him at the hospital.

Rose's body was wracked by sobs.

She didn't feel Damon move at first because of it.

Then she realized her hands were moving without her.

Rose held her breath and looked down.

Damon was coughing, water spewing from his mouth.

Then his eyes opened.

Rose let out a breath that absolutely shook.

Then she was scrambling to her feet.

"Don't move, help is on the way," she yelled down at him.

Rose stumbled her way up and away from the pond and ran to the patio with everything she had.

Then everything she had quickly met a wall.

She blinked into the impact before realizing it was her wall.

James said something—she was sure of it—but she didn't hear a word.

Rose collapsed against him.

His arms were warm and strong as they held her up.

In the last week—in the last day—the world had gotten loud, messy and complicated.

But right then, Rose felt only him.

NIGHT FINALLY FELL.

The Seven Roads Motel was empty again. James's house was not.

Sheriff Weaver's badge was on his hip, but his hands were around a beer. It had been offered to him once his shift had officially ended. He hadn't had any sip of it, but then again, James also hadn't had a drink of his either. Instead, they were on the back porch looking out at the field of tall grass.

They had been sitting in silence a bit while they waited for the sheriff's wife to finish seeing about Rose. Both women were upstairs in the guest bedroom. Without being asked the men had given them space.

That morning had been a lot.

Now they were all trying to wind down.

Though there were still concerns. Weaver seemed to guess at James's main ones. He spoke into the night air with a tiredness that James couldn't deny he felt a bit too.

"The doctors say Damon might not wake up at all, but if he does, he has a detail on him until we get a better sense of what's what," he said. "But Darius and I agree, we think there's nothing else out there waiting for Rose. Whatever conflict went on between Damon and Lloyd, it seemed to put a stop to whatever might have come next. Still, it might not be a bad idea to let her stay with you a few more days."

No one could make Rose do what she didn't want.

That said, James had already decided he wasn't going to let the deputy be alone. Whether that meant her staying at his house or him camping outside of her apartment, he was more than prepared to follow her lead.

But he wasn't about to say that to her boss. Not without her okaying it.

Instead, James nodded.

"I'll look after her," he promised.

Weaver was pleased. He scratched at the label on his bottle. James felt his eyes on him but kept his gaze ahead. James bet the sheriff was wondering about the two of them—Rose and James. Weaver had been the first to arrive at the groundskeeper's house and the first to see Rose, completely folded into his arms.

She hadn't moved from that position until the EMTs had arrived and insisted on checking both of them. That was when she had finally seen the blood on his sleeves.

"Is that blood?" she had asked, strength zipping through her tears. "Are you hurt?"

He had smiled down at her but felt no joy in it.

"It's not mine."

He'd told them about Lloyd then, upstairs in that room. There was no saving him, and when Rose had finally left his side to talk to a newly arrived Price, James had told the sheriff everything Lloyd had said.

Almost everything.

"If you want this to end here, I suggest you don't repeat what I'm about to say..."

If Lloyd had acted any differently, if he hadn't seemed so sincere, James wouldn't have omitted anything from the sheriff or Detective Williams. Yet, he couldn't find anything to doubt in the man's warning.

So James kept Lloyd's last words to himself. If there was any chance it could keep Rose safe, he was going to take it for now.

Maybe that was what Sheriff Weaver suspected now. Maybe he knew James was withholding something. Or maybe he was just tired.

He let out a long breath and turned back toward the field.

"I think it might rain this week," he said after a moment.

James turned his bottle around in his hand, the condensation wetting his fingers.

"We could use just a little of it," he said.

"That we could," Weaver agreed.

They sat in silence, not a bad one, until Blake appeared at the back door. She had one hand on her belly and the other reaching for her husband.

"It's time for us to go to sleep," she told him. Then to James, "You too, Mr. Keller."

Both men stood.

"How's Rose doing?" the sheriff asked.

Blake looked caught between sad and okay.

"She'll be okay. She just needs some time to process, is all." A smile lit her face. She spoke softly to her husband, but James was reassured by it too. "Don't worry. Wildcard Rose will be back after a good, well-deserved rest."

That cheering outlook led the three of them back through the house to the front porch. The sheriff said he would check in on them the next day while Blake encouraged James to focus on keeping Rose at home for a bit.

"That girl can roll with a lot of punches but staying put to heal from them has never been her strong suit," Blake added. "Not to step out of line here, but I don't think she'd mind healing if you were staying put right there with her."

James told her not to worry. He'd make sure she got the rest she needed. Then the Weavers locked hands and walked slowly to their car. He couldn't hear everything they said but he spied them looking up at the stars together.

He turned off the porch light to give them some privacy.

James had only spent one night away from his house, but it felt like a lifetime ago. He went through each room, checking every inch to make sure everything was like it had been.

Then he came to a stop at the guest bedroom door.

It was open enough that James could make out Rose, lying in the bed.

She was facing away from him, wrapped up in a quilt.

James had already told her good-night, knowing she was exhausted, and she had returned the sentiment, eyes swollen and heavy. So there was no reason for him to go in to see her now. No reason to talk to her. No reason to be near her.

He could go to his own room across the hall and probably fall asleep in a wink.

Yet, James couldn't move from his spot at the door.

She was safe now.

His house was safe.

There was no reason to worry. There was no reason to hover. There was no—

James pushed open the door and walked around the side of the bed. Rose opened her eyes to the sound. She didn't say a word as she watched him.

She didn't say a thing as he took the covers off her.

She didn't make a sound as he scooped her up into his arms, her side against his chest and bare legs dangling freely while he walked her out of the guest bedroom and across the hall.

Instead, she let him place her directly into his bed, watched him get in beside her, and accepted the covers he pulled up over them both. He reached up and clicked the light off and kept that silence going until a few minutes passed.

Then, he told her something he had never told another soul.

"When I was a kid, I got into a really bad fight with a teenager in the same foster home as me. He was pushing around a girl in the home with us and I tried to protect her. I did some damage to him but I was just a little thing and I had to have two surgeries on my arm. I had nightmares after that, recurring bad ones that carried on for years. I'd wake up screaming and crying, and sometimes when it got really bad, I'd just completely shut down until morning. When that happened, no one could get me talking. It was like I was dead to the world. Everyone thought the nightmares were from the fight and the surgeries and getting moved around from foster home to foster home, but it wasn't any of that."

He couldn't see her but knew Rose was looking up at him from her pillow. He took a breath and told her the secret he had kept since he was six.

"The thing that scared me the most was when I woke up in the hospital after my surgery. It was night, the room was dark, and I was alone. And I stayed that way for maybe twenty minutes before a nurse came in to do her rounds. But that twenty minutes? It felt like a lifetime times two. Small, hurt, and in the dark without any idea of what my future looked like. I didn't know if I was okay, I didn't know if I was in trouble, and the worst part, I didn't know if anyone cared about me either." James could still feel that terror, those fears that had him frozen in that hospital bed until a nurse came in. "Since then, I have spent every day working on making a life that never puts me in that situation again. Making sure I can one day help other kids never feel that too. And I think I've done a good job of it so far. I can sleep by myself in a dark room and not worry about a thing. But I'm here to tell you something right now, Rose Little."

He rolled onto his side to face her.

He imagined her dark eyes searching him but could only make out her silhouette now.

Even that brought him comfort.

"For the first time in my life, the idea of falling asleep alone bothered me more than waking up by myself. So, if you don't mind, I'd like you to stay with me tonight. At least until I fall asleep, just so I can know you're here. So I can know that you're safe. If that's okay with you."

In the dark Rose Little said four words.

"It's okay with me."

Her hand went beneath the covers and found his. She interlocked their fingers together and, a few minutes later, she was asleep.

James listened to her even breathing, felt the warmth of her hand in his, and smiled into the darkness.

Finally, he let out that breath he had felt like he'd been holding all day.

Then, he slept.

Chapter Seventeen

Rose had never had a problem falling asleep. She had never felt fear at waking up either. For all her life, she had been fortunate enough to not worry about the before and after of something she had clearly taken for granted.

When she opened her eyes the next morning, Rose felt appreciation for the warmth in her. Because of the warmth next to her.

James Keller was a big, scary man at first glance. Tall and wide and muscled, eyes sharp and clear, words low and often concise. He wore coveralls coated in oil and grime, lived in an isolated old house, and when he wasn't smiling, he looked like he was forever uninterested.

But boy, how different he was to Rose now.

She looked up at the sleeping face resting next to her. She had fallen asleep facing him, hand in his, and now she woke up in the same position. James was on his side, facing her, his arm outstretched and resting softly on her hip while the other was tucked beneath his cheek.

Despite his intimidating appearance, Rose saw the softness in him.

He cared and he was loud with it. He was quiet with it.

He held her, carried her and stayed by her side.

This man whom she had known less than two weeks.

This man whom she had continuously endangered.

But had he ever complained?

Had he ever blamed her?

Not even when his family's shop had burned down.

Not when he'd been hurt getting her out of the debris.

And definitely not when he had waited at her side in the hospital to wake up after.

Rose felt her cheeks heat at the memory.

"I have a thing about hospitals," he had told her then. "When I was a kid, I woke up in one alone and it really did a number on me. Now I try to make sure that it doesn't happen to others if I can."

Rose had heard about James's backstory enough to know about the fight that had landed him in the hospital, but that had been it. She hadn't known that he had woken up alone, in the dark, feeling unloved. And that was why he had stayed with her then, a stranger.

He didn't want her to wake up alone.

The warmth in Rose's cheeks spread to her chest. She became less aware of how intimate they were in their closeness and instead focused on how she felt.

A few minutes later, she finally understood.

But when James started to stir, she decided to keep it to herself for a while.

As much as she appreciated the soft and warm, the last twenty-four hours—and honestly, the past several days—were still sitting heavy.

Especially now that she had a safe space to think on it all.

"You know, we could sleep in, and no one would

care." James's eyes were still closed but his lips twitched like he wanted to smile.

Rose rolled her eyes on reflex. She eyed the window on the other side of the room.

"Tell that to your lack of blackout curtains," she said. "I may be able to do a lot of things but sleeping in the sun only works for cat naps."

James let out a little laugh and, in sync, the two of them stretched. His arm lifted from her hip, then they both rolled onto their backs like it was a daily routine.

"I've been meaning to get some, but I'm usually up and at the shop by six," he said. "Once I took over the shop's day-to-day I realized it was easier to get some stuff done before it actually opened and before Mr. Donahue showed and got to chatting." He folded his pillow to prop himself up. "Also, to be fair, no one's complained about the lack of curtains, so I keep putting it off."

Rose's eyebrow went up. She was about to ask how many people he had had in his room when the man cleared his throat.

"Which would definitely be because no one has ever stayed in my room before," he clarified before she could ask. "Just in case you were wondering."

Rose held in her smile but didn't comment past that.

"There's nothing to be shy about, Mr. Keller," she teased. "We've all lived a life before now."

What they were doing now felt normal.

What had happened the day before didn't.

Rose doubled back.

"It's Damon and Lloyd's lives now that I don't understand." The tone shifted, and so did they. Rose sat up and James mimicked the move. Whatever warmth they had shared just being in one another's company the night before chilled into calculations.

"Yesterday there was…a lot going on and I don't think I really talked about how much of it bothered me. I mean the reasoning behind what had happened."

Rose had given Liam, and by extension James since he hadn't left her side once until they had gotten to his house, a play-by-play of everything that had been said and happened once Lloyd appeared on the dock. She had been matter-of-fact with the retelling. Now she was looking at the overall story.

"So, Lloyd came down the dock, Damon threw his gun into the water, and then tied me to the cinder block, all without talking. Lloyd tied Damon to the other one after that. Then Lloyd shot him and walked off. Just like that." It had felt like watching a bizarre movie. One left on mute until the gun went off and the force had pushed Damon's body back into the water. "And, while I have a lot of questions from all of that, Damon allowing himself to be shot is what gets me.

"He talked about being betrayed by someone he loves, but how was he betrayed?" she continued. "He had a gun, he had time, he had drive, and yet, he just gave in. Threw his weapon away, let his feet be tied to concrete, and even let Lloyd help him to the edge of the dock before he was shot. And James, he *smiled* while it happened." She shook her head, unable to shake the image. "With me, Damon was angry. Full of rage. Then, at what he thought would be his death, he accepted it with what felt like happiness?"

She held up another finger, deciding she had enough questions to tick off points.

"Which leads me to the Lloyd of it all. You said he talked about heroes and how he understood now why Damon had been so angry. Then he killed himself? Why? Did he betray Damon? And what exactly *was* the betrayal? Getting me to the dock to try and kill me only for Lloyd to come out and take on Damon instead? If that's true, then why didn't he fight back? Why did Lloyd just leave and do himself in like that? Why—"

Rose had been ticking off her points haphazardly. She had nine fingers up and was going for ten. James interrupted the move.

He took both of her hands in only one of his and pushed all three to the space on the bed between them.

She turned to meet his gaze. Green, brown and her new favorite, gold, took her in as quickly as his hand had.

"Sometimes, we just don't get all of the answers." His voice was deep velvet. Smooth, soft. "And the answers we do get, we might not get all at once."

He squeezed the top of her hands.

"Whatever went down yesterday, it was the end of something so why don't we honor that with starting something new today?"

Despite herself, Rose felt her eyebrow go sky-high.

"Something new?" she asked, mind pausing the merry-go-round of questions she had. "Like what?"

Belatedly, Rose realized just how close they were.

James's lips turned up at the corners.

"Come downstairs and you'll see."

A few minutes later Rose met James in the kitchen.

There was coffee made and breakfast in progress. She sat dutifully at the eat-in kitchen table, waiting for their something new to start. James, however, didn't explain and started to talk about a TV show Mr. Donahue had told him about while he finished cooking.

Rose tried to stay on task but found the conversation distracting. When he added his famous stuffed omelets? She forgot to ask again. Later, after they had moved to the couch to watch the show, she thought again about what he'd meant. That question was replaced again by idle chatter between them.

A few hours later, they were walking through the field behind the house, Rose following him as James talked about his goals for fixing up the house. He had some landscaping ideas too for the front of the lot, but he didn't seem keen on ever changing the back. At least not the tall grass they were moving through. He reached down on occasion to touch the grass, like a parent affectionately patting the head of their child.

Around then Rose thought about what he had meant by starting something new.

She ran her hand across the top of the grass and followed him instead.

She didn't ask again.

THREE DAYS WENT by like that.

Simple days that were neither eventful nor boring.

They ate together, watched TV together, went on walks around the property together, and when it was time to sleep, they did that together too.

The first night this happened, they both used excuses of still being wary of everything that had been going on. The second night, those excuses were given with much less enthusiasm. The third night, it felt like habit.

James moved the covers for Rose to get in first—while she talked about whatever throwaway topic they had landed on for that moment—and then got into bed himself once she was settled. He nodded and mmm-hmmed at all the right places while plugging his phone in to charge and Rose put on her hand lotion before handing it over to him. They kept their conversations going until the lights were off, but even after, they carried on for a few more minutes.

They fell asleep without touching, but that never held true for the mornings.

James always had an arm around or on her. Rose always had her face resting on him or against him while wrapped around his arm or leg. Or both, just as she had in the motel room.

And they never talked about it. Even as they detangled in the morning, neither one of them stated the obvious.

Or questioned why they weren't questioning it.

Those three days and nights became routine. Comfortable and safe.

So when Doc Ernest's daughter Lily called her the morning of the fourth day, Rose couldn't help but feel a sense of loss.

"You told me to let you know if Damon Tillman had any visitors, and one finally showed up," Lily said. "She's talking to the doctor right now."

"She?" Rose lowered her voice so James couldn't overhear her from the kitchen. It was his turn to do the dishes.

Lily also lowered her voice.

"Yeah," she said. "And she seems really upset."

Damon had been moved out of the ICU the day before, but as far as Rose knew, he hadn't woken up yet. And he might not. She hadn't gotten any more updates about him or the case since Liam and Blake had left the night they had brought Rose and James back. Rose, however, had reached out to Lily before James had swayed her into taking a break from everything.

Lily's answer had put her right back onto all her questions, all her concerns.

Rose came back to herself with guilt riding shotgun.

That guilt carried her to look into the kitchen.

James looked no less mighty rinsing dishes.

She could stand there, stand in that house, and be with him, and while the rest of the world went about its own business, she could be happy. Be content.

But she wouldn't be Deputy Rose Little.

"If she starts to leave, try and stall her," she told Lily. "I'm on the way."

Chapter Eighteen

The woman was young. She was also very, very sad.

"That's Wynonna Harrison, Lloyd Harrison's little sister," Price whispered at her side. "She came in yesterday to handle everything for Lloyd but is here for Damon today."

Rose and Price were inside Lane Medical lurking in a hallway, watching the young woman fiddle with the vending machine down the hall from Damon's room. An even younger deputy named Cameron was sitting in plain clothes on the bench next to his door. The department was on rotation to keep an eye on the suspect until the case could be officially closed.

"Hospital security is nice but Damon took on one of our own, so the sheriff wanted the department to handle it," Price had told her earlier in the car as they drove from the house to the hospital.

Price had agreed to give her the ride to and from as a favor to their friendship since she wasn't allowed back to work until the next day. Even though she had been resting—something Rose Little never did—he understood better than most that sometimes you had to see something all the way through before you could stop looking at it. That friendship and understanding, though, apparently had limits.

"I have a feeling James wouldn't be too happy about you sneaking away to go see the man who's been trying to kill you," he had said, flatly.

Rose had rolled her eyes.

"I'm not sneaking and I'm not going to see Damon either," she had responded. "I'm going to see the *person* who is seeing Damon. Plus, last I heard Damon hasn't woken up yet."

Price hadn't seemed all that convinced.

"All I'm saying is that I'm not lying to James about where we're going, so I'll stay in the car while you figure it out."

Rose had taken offense to that.

"Who said I have to lie to him? I'm a grown woman. I can go where I want."

She had stayed true to that word. She hadn't lied to James about where she was going. She had simply decided to leave him a note instead.

It wasn't like she *was* doing anything wrong. And she *was* a grown woman after all, but somehow she felt a whole lot of guilt for going. Doubly so that she hadn't asked him to come too.

She had tried to reason with herself that it was because James had already been through so much because of her. He didn't need to do the technical parts like tying up loose ends too.

Was this even a loose end, though?

Rose watched as the young Wynonna bought a drink. After she took the can, she stayed standing right there.

"Hey, why don't you take Cameron to the cafeteria?"

Rose said to Price. "They finished fixing it up already. I'll even give you some cash to throw around."

Price snorted.

"Spot me a ten and we're in business, Little."

She did but Rose knew he wouldn't actually spend it. In all of the years of their friendship, he'd never taken her money. Just her barbs and stubbornness. Rose decided one day she should thank him for being such a good friend. Until then she waited for him to lead Cameron away and then walked over to meet Wynonna before she could go back inside.

Rose could see the red-rimmed eyes, the tiredness. She also saw recognition.

"You're Deputy Little," she said.

Rose gave her a polite smile.

"I am. And you're Wynonna Harrison? Lloyd's sister?"

If there was any resentment or anger or worry about Rose, someone who had been a strange part—but a part nonetheless—in her brother's death, she didn't show in. On the contrary, she also seemed polite.

"I am," she said with a nod. "And I was really hoping to find you. Could we talk?"

They sat in the bench seats next to Damon's door. The room next to it and across the hall were empty and the staff had just finished their rounds. The two women were alone for now.

And they both made quick use of that privacy, starting with Wynonna.

"I've already heard what the sheriff had to say and the detective too, but I'd really like to hear from you what happened the day my brother—" she stopped herself and took a breath before continuing "—the other day. If you don't mind."

Rose didn't.

She told the woman everything that had happened, leaving no details out. There was no way to soften the impact of Lloyd's death, but Rose had seen enough in her career to know that having the whole story could help the loved ones left behind move on.

And Rose wanted that for Wynonna because she obviously had been very close to her brother.

When Rose was done with her retelling of the events she had gone through, the younger Harrison was drying her eyes with a tissue she had pulled from her pocket.

Rose was going to give her some time before starting in with some of the questions she had and was thinking of offering to go get the younger woman something to drink or eat, when Wynonna shook her head.

"This doesn't make sense. None of this makes sense."

Rose's attention snapped back to her like a rubber band.

"What do you mean?" she asked.

Wynonna put her tissue down and angled her body to face Rose more directly. Her brow knitted together as she spoke.

"They said that they think Lloyd killed himself because Damon was threatening him with something but then Lloyd was able to get the upper hand last minute. But Damon would never do that. Not to Lloyd. Just like Lloyd would never do that. Not to Damon."

Rose's confusion must have shown on her expression.

Wynonna stopped.

"I'm sorry but why wouldn't Damon hurt Lloyd?" Rose asked. "You make it sound like they were close."

The other woman responded with no space between. "They were."

Wynonna looked as bewildered by the question as Rose felt about the answer.

"Damon and Lloyd were close?" Rose had to clarify.

Wynonna nodded.

"Since they were kids, or teenagers, really. You didn't know?"

Rose didn't. After Derrick had passed, she had only ever seen Damon and once Damon had started to attack her, the only information they had found about him had been basic. He lived alone, not married, no kids. He was a consultant for a business that Rose had never really paid attention to.

Why would she have?

It had been so cut-and-dried.

Damon blamed her for Derrick's death, and he wanted revenge.

Lloyd had seemed like a simple addition to that plan.

"I had no idea."

Wynonna looked down at her phone. She let out a breath.

"There's actually a pretty big age gap between me and Lloyd," she started. "We weren't actually that close because of it until our mom died. Our dad was a truck driver and never really home, so Lloyd kind of took over as my parent. Then one day our dad just never came home. If that wasn't enough kicks to the teeth, I got really sick when I was twelve. That's the first time I met Damon."

Wynonna ran her thumb over her phone screen. She kept staring down at it, but Rose suspected she was seeing a memory instead.

"They had just graduated high school and instead of going off to college and doing normal things eighteen-year-olds would do, they got jobs at a local restaurant and paid for my treatment. One would work day shift and the other nights and the same went for staying with me." A smile briefly passed over her lips. "A nurse complained once that it always smelled like fried chicken and alcohol in my room."

Wynonna looked up as a couple walked across the end of their hallway. The reality of where they were must have sobered her.

Her head lowered again.

"That's how I grew up, though. From twelve until eighteen I had two brothers, two best friends, two parents. Whatever you want to call them, they were always there. Day in and day out. The big stuff and the little stuff. For seven years I saw Lloyd and Damon every day, and after that, I saw them during breaks from school. Holidays, special events. My college graduation. And if one of them couldn't make it because of work, the other always showed. I was *never* alone because of them. Never. Not once. Their love for me? For each other? For our little family? Has been the best part of my life. And now? Now I'm being told that Damon was betrayed by Lloyd? That Lloyd tried to kill Damon? Then himself because of some unknown reason?"

Tears had started to fall down the woman's cheeks. They were full of frustration.

"I'll never ever believe that," she said. "And if you had seen them together, you wouldn't either."

Her frustration devolved into sorrow. She pulled more tissues out of her pocket and sobbed into them with palpable feeling.

Rose didn't ask any more questions after that.

For one, no matter what Lloyd had done, his sister mourning him was a separate matter altogether. She deserved peace. Rose wasn't going to beat through that to answer her curiosity.

And secondly, Rose believed she had the answer she had wanted most.

Why had Damon and Lloyd been so gentle with such violent acts? Why had Damon let himself be tied up and then shot without an ounce of fight in him? Why had Lloyd, the one who had seemingly beaten the bad guy, walked away only to end his own life?

The answer was something Rose had never even considered as a possibility.

Love.

That was why Damon had smiled like that, even at what he believed would be his end.

Which meant that their last stands made no sense… unless someone else was forcing their hands.

Normally, Rose would have wondered what could force two men to abandon their plans of revenge and their love for one another so quickly and in complete agreement.

But after hearing Wynonna praise Damon, Lloyd and their little family, and Rose was absolutely certain of the answer now.

It was her.

Someone had threatened Wynonna, their sister, their best friend, their child.

And so they had gladly gone to death.

Rose watched the young woman cry.

She had come to the hospital with questions in hopes of getting answers to help her move on. To put closure between her and Damon Tillman's violent attempts to take her life.

When Rose left later, she left with a new purpose burning a hole through her chest.

She was going to find the third man.

And she was going to make him pay for what he had done.

THE WEATHER WAS done being fickle. The heat and humidity gave way to rain just a half hour before Rose came back. It wasn't a big downpour, but it wasn't a misting either. It would have watered the flowers, had James bought and planted them.

He sat on the front porch, looking out at spots he had been thinking about starting a garden. Never a man with a green thumb, but he thought he'd do fine enough with the simple flowers.

He was sitting there on the front porch, arms crossed over his chest, when Price's cruiser drove down the driveway.

James stood and grabbed the umbrella he had leaned up against the wall next to him. He opened it with purpose; he walked to the passenger's door with frustration.

Rose's gaze was downcast when the door came open. Price called across the seat to him.

"I wanted to get her home before the rain, but it snuck

up on us. Looks like it might keep up until tomorrow afternoon. Nothing too bad, though."

James felt his jaw clench but didn't direct his ire at the deputy, especially since he had been the one to give a follow-up call to him once they had gotten to the hospital.

"The more I think about the way she was acting, I'm not so sure Rose told you where we were going," Price had said. "With everything that's been going on, I figured you might be a little more worried than the rest, so I wanted to make sure you knew she was okay."

James had thanked him and they had ended the call. The keys James had had in his hand stayed there until he finally put them back on the hook.

The note James had found on his bed had indeed said she was going to take care of a few things with Price. But that had been it. No other details and, when he had called her, her phone had kept ringing until getting to voicemail.

Price had timed his own call well.

James had been ready to drive out and search for the woman before it had come in.

He had been relieved.

Now he was grumpy.

Rose must have sensed the mood.

"Thanks for the ride, Price," she said, a little louder than what felt like normal. Instead of waiting for a reply she was out of the car and hurrying to the house.

James nodded to Price before easily catching up.

He thought he heard laughing behind him, but James's focus had only one aim now.

When they got to the porch, James lowered the umbrella and shook it out.

Rose was smart. She used the time to escape inside.

Four of her quick steps, though, was a lazy two steps for him.

Rose made it to the living room and only had enough time to turn around and face him, hands up in defense.

"Listen, before you say anything, I know I should have talked to you before I just up and left but—"

She might have been a whole lot smaller than him, but in that moment, her lips were an easy reach.

James felt Rose stiffen against his kiss but he wasn't intending to prolong it.

Not without saying exactly what was on his mind first.

James pulled away but only enough to give space to his words.

"Rose Little, I'm mad at you."

Chapter Nineteen

He held her chin, tilting it up to catch those hazel eyes she had grown so familiar with. That didn't mean they couldn't confuse her from time to time, like now.

Rose blinked up at the giant man who had just interrupted her with a kiss.

"Excuse me?"

James didn't retract his words. Instead, he doubled down.

"I'm mad at you, Rose Little. I'm mad that you left without saying anything and I'm mad that you didn't answer my call. I mean, even Deputy Collins felt like I deserve some kind of check-in to know you're okay after everything you've been through. That we've been through. I know you're Wildcard Rose but sometimes I think you use that as a pass to run headlong into danger and it's okay." He shook his head, truly looking the part of a man angry at having been left in the dark.

Rose started to say something—she wasn't sure what—when he continued.

"And that's what I thought I was mad about before you got here. You, being you, running into the unknown swinging. But then I saw you and I realized I'm really just mad at me. I'm mad I didn't give you a good reason for you to take me with you. So I'm going to make sure I give it now."

That frown didn't lessen but his words seemed to soften.

"I like you, Rose Little," he said. "I want to be with you whether we're eating breakfast, talking about TV, or surviving explosions in service pits. I don't need you to stop being Wildcard Rose. I just want to be by your side when you're doing it. I want to help you, I want to fight for you and with you. I want to do the hard stuff and the boring stuff. I want to finally tell Mr. Donahue I officially can't date his daughter because some loud woman one day pulled up into my garage without an appointment and then told me she couldn't just leave me alone."

He finally smiled.

"I want your good news and your bad news, Rose Little. I want your chaos and your calm. I want—"

The man sure was talkative. That was what Rose was thinking when the last vestige of her self-control finally snapped.

It was her turn to do the interrupting and interrupting she sure did.

Rose threw her arms around James's neck and fastened the two of them together. She started with their lips and then folded against him with every curve and surface of her body that she could.

If James was mad at the cutoff, he certainly didn't stay that way.

His tongue was hungry, and it parted her lips in unison with his hands running down her sides. It was light work after that.

James cupped her backside in his hands and had her airborne in a second flat. Like they had rehearsed the move, Rose wrapped her legs around his waist, all without breaking their kiss.

If anything, the new position made the pace even more frenzied.

James made surprisingly quick work of getting them from the living room to the second-floor bedroom in one heavy-breathing journey. And he did so in a way that only stoked the fire within Rose higher.

He had her horizontal two steps inside of the bedroom, careful to cushion her body from the drop down.

Sadly, the move ended their kiss.

Luckily, it gave him the space to do something even more riveting.

James Keller was already a handsome, good-looking man, but the second he rid himself of his clothes, Rose knew something else to be just as true.

His height wasn't the only big thing about him.

Rose couldn't help but stare a little longer than she originally meant to. James noticed and let out a laugh.

"I've got good news and I've got bad news," he said, his fingers working the last of her clothes down her legs.

Rose struggled to keep her composure as cold air started to hit all the right spots.

"What—what is it?"

James didn't smile. He smirked.

"Good news is, I'm about to spend a good amount of time with you in this bed, Deputy." To emphasize his plans, he brought his naked body flush with hers and moved his fingers down between her legs.

Rose gasped in surprise and felt her breathing quicken from a new kind of pleasure.

James's gaze went from hers and then down to her lips. He pushed deep inside of her and watched as her mouth opened in appreciation.

Then he laughed again.

"Do you want to know the bad news?"

He picked up the pace and all Rose could do was manage a nod.

Still, he didn't answer right away. At least not with words.

He hit the right spot and worked it until Rose's body bucked up against him in a dazzling twist of release. It wasn't until he captured her mouth in his and devoured her a little longer there, that he moved himself to the part of Rose that wanted him most.

His words weren't warm or soft. They weren't gentle or quiet.

They were hot and they were ready.

"The bad news is, I do believe you might be sore in the morning."

Without any more teasing or talking, he thrust inside of her with a nearly overwhelming force.

Nearly.

Rose took him in with a moan that would have made her grateful that house was empty.

That moan was one of many that afternoon as his good news really did pan out. They stayed tangled in his sheets until the sun started to set. Once they had exhausted themselves and Rose lay there trying to catch her breath back, she already knew he would be right about the bad news.

Though, to her, what she had just done with James could never be counted as bad.

A belief she took into that night when round two started up in the shower.

By the time they had found themselves truly, truly exhausted and back in bed, Rose didn't have the stamina or focus to remember what it was she wanted to talk about with James before this all had started.

Maybe if she had, what happened next might have gone a whole lot differently.

JAMES ADDED A set of blackout curtains to his online shopping cart the second after he woke up the next morning. The sun wasn't completely out—the rain was being lazy in its walk across Seven Roads—but there was enough of it to make Rose start stirring from her own sleep.

James hovered his hands over her eyes, cutting off a beam that was particularly precise, but it wasn't enough to keep her in her dreams.

Rose's eyes fluttered opened a minute or two into his attempt. When she saw his hand, though, she only laughed.

"Not even the mighty James Keller can compete with the morning sun."

James felt the vibration of her stretching out her legs before that vibration ran up to her arms. She didn't go for the normal starfish pose since she, as per her usual habits over the last several days, was already wrapped tightly around his bicep.

She shook him lightly, then became nosy about his phone.

"Don't tell me you're the kind of man who shops online all of the time, even in bed."

James snorted.

"Only when I'm buying the necessities," he countered. He held his phone closer so she could see it more clearly. "I *am* the kind of man to be generous, though. Need me to get anything for you? Say the word."

Rose rubbed her forehead against his arm as she shook her head.

"I'm pretty happy with what I have already, thanks."

James wasn't sure if that was a nod to him, but he felt the warmth of it anyways. Confessing his feelings to the deputy the day before had been a spur-of-the-moment decision made from a spur-of-the-moment realization. But he didn't regret it. He certainly didn't regret what had come after either.

Now, however, he was realizing that Rose hadn't returned those feelings. At least not in words.

But who was he to nitpick?

Surely she felt enough of something for him to do what they had done multiple times the day before. He didn't need the words.

At least not now.

"I'm starting to think you're a pretty relaxed woman. At least, when not on the clock. Then again, I still have never seen someone as calm as you when you were staring down at a seat covering a bomb."

James regretted the mention as soon as he said it. He didn't want to remind Rose of the close calls they had encountered, not when the last week had been so kind to them, but he felt her tense and knew it was already too late. The damage was done, and the damage was Rose pulling away from him.

"I'm sorry," he hurried. "I didn't mean to bring any of that stuff up. It's just one of those once-in-a-lifetime things I can't believe happened."

She shook her head.

"It's not that. I just realized I haven't told you what I found out yesterday."

And that was when James learned about Wynonna Harrison and her brother's past with Damon.

"Before I left, Wynonna told me that even though Damon helped raise her with Lloyd, Derrick only visited on occasion," she added at the end of the retelling. "Derrick and Lloyd were friendly but not at all like Damon and Lloyd. They *were* close enough, though, that when there was a position open after Lloyd was hired into Camden Pharmaceuticals, he reached out to Derrick, who was looking for a job. That's how the two of them came to be on that bus five months ago while Damon wasn't around."

"And no one knew about Lloyd's relationship with Derrick's brother?"

Rose said no.

"I'm guessing they probably wanted to avoid any conflicts at work or about how Derrick got the job. Though I guess I don't know for sure. Just like I'm still not sure why the two of them were fighting on the bus, especially during a tornado." Rose's face scrunched up. "Or why Derrick would look so hateful at a man that his brother obviously loved very much."

She fell into a silence while she probably was thinking about the possibilities.

James, on the other hand, realized he had reason to apologize now.

"At the time I thought keeping it quiet was the right play but I'm not sure that's the case anymore." Rose's eyes widened. "I'm sorry I should have told you this sooner."

It was James's turn to recount a conversation. His was all about Lloyd, up in that second-story room before he had taken his own life.

Rose wasn't angry at his omission. She seemed to be enthused by it.

"The day Derrick died he stopped calling Damon a hero," she paraphrased. "It wasn't my fault that Derrick died. It was the storm… The generator."

Rose rocketed upright.

It was so sudden James sat up next.

She turned to him and spoke fast and with her hands too.

"The generator. The damned generator. It was supposed to be the top-of-the-line and kick on no matter what. But it didn't that day. That's why they got on the shuttle in the first place. 'One single point of failure' that messed up everything."

James started to pick up what she was putting down.

"Lloyd was doing something and the power going out messed it up. That means he was probably doing something he shouldn't have at the research annex? And Derrick found out?"

"Something that must have included Damon and

that's why he was so mad at Lloyd," Rose jumped in. "That's why he stopped calling Damon a hero."

Rose didn't wait to finish the conversation. She was scurrying out of bed in her underthings, quickly searching out a fresh pair of clothes.

James followed suit, though he didn't know exactly what they were going to do next.

Rose continued once she had a pair of jeans in hand.

"If Damon and Lloyd were working together to do something illegal at the drug trial, then them turning on one another like that would make sense, if they *both* hadn't been ready to die." She pointed at him, jeans waving through the air in the process. "*But* what if there was a third person in on it? Someone who knew enough to know where to hurt them."

James found a shirt and tugged it on, heart starting to beat a little bit faster. Her excitement at a possible breakthrough was oddly contagious.

"But why get you there for the end of it?" he asked. "Or do you think Damon just got interrupted during his revenge plot against you?"

Rose did a combo between a headshake and a shrug.

"I'm not sure but maybe Wynonna has more information about Lloyd's time at Camden," she said. "Maybe she can remember something that we can—"

Rose stopped herself as her phone started to vibrate on the nightstand.

She hurried over and made a little noise after she scanned the new alert.

"It's a text from Cameron… Oh my God."

"What?"

James was at her side in a flash, as if he could somehow fight the phone if needed.

It wasn't good news and it wasn't bad news.

But it was shocking news.

"Damon Tillman is awake."

Chapter Twenty

There was still one thing that was bothering Rose, and for the life of her, she couldn't catch the thought. It bothered her like a small pebble caught in her shoe. No matter how many times she tried to shake it out, it stayed.

It rubbed.

It annoyed.

She felt James's gaze fall on her. After the elevator doors closed behind them, he finally asked if she was okay.

Rose couldn't decide, so she did a half shrug and head tilt.

"I'm not sure," she admitted. "There's…something I'm forgetting? But I'm not even sure where there's space to have forgotten something. We've gone over every question with an answer now or at least a confirmation that we still need an answer. Nothing has been left undone, right?"

She faced him full-on and took a tiny step forward. It put her close enough that she had to crane her head back to look up at him while he tilted his forward to look down at her.

If she hadn't been so focused on trying to solve her

problem, she thought she might blush at the closeness. Especially since James had been right—she *was* sore from their previous trysts between the sheets.

As it was, she gave him the most serious of expressions to know she meant business.

"Or *do* we have any other outlying questions? Things we were trying to answer before what happened out at the cemetery?"

James turned thoughtful.

"The only other thing I was wondering about was how much trouble was I going to get into for basically stealing a car from someone at this very same hospital last week." He shrugged. "But the car wasn't damaged and the sheriff sweet-talked that guy into forgiving me since he knew him. So that's that for me."

Rose stifled a smile, despite herself.

The man whose car James had taken was bingo buddies with Liam's newest father-in-law. Rose still was waiting for the time to ask him about how *that* conversation had gone. She bet Blake had also gotten a good kick out of it.

But Rose was still feeling *bothered.*

The elevator arrived at its destination. The doors slid open but Rose didn't move from her spot yet.

"There's *something*," she reiterated. "And it's really bugging me."

James reached down and put a thumb between her eyebrows. He pressed the crinkled skin there, gently.

"Don't worry, Little," he said. "I believe in you. You'll get there."

It was a simple pep talk but it did the trick. Rose decided to try and shake off the feeling and come back to it later when she had the mental space for it. In her experience not every detail always shook out. Sometimes you had to eventually just walk away.

Or sometimes the thing that's bothering you walks into your elevator.

No sooner had the doors slid open than a man nearly bowled her over.

Her reflexes were normally spitfire-fast, but James beat her this time. His large hand wrapped easily around her hip before tugging her back. She thudded softly against his chest, a wall of muscle she now knew in the most intimate of senses.

"Excuse me," the newcomer offered. He kept his face on the control panel but offered a lackluster nod in their direction. Rose narrowed her eyes at him while James told him it was no problem.

That was when she saw the cast on his arm.

The rest of the details synced up.

Rose knew this person. At least enough to recognize him.

It was the reporter.

The man she had met the day of the explosion. Why had she never learned his name?

He didn't make eye contact. Rose was grateful for it. The last thing she needed was to have to deal with the media at the moment. A member of the media who obviously had a distaste for her based on their last interaction.

James pushed her forward before the doors could close. Rose allowed it, eyes still narrowed. That bothered feeling stayed as they walked away and down the hallway toward Damon's room.

She had bigger fish to fry, after all. With Damon being awake they could hopefully get some answers and find a new direction to go in to find who had actually been pulling the strings.

But nothing had been that simple so far and that theme continued on.

Deputy Cameron wasn't sitting outside.

No one from the department was.

Wynonna also wasn't there. Not at the bench and not in front of the vending machines.

"The vending machines."

Rose stopped. That piece that had been missing. That pebble in her shoe.

The dang vending machines.

James's eyebrow rose.

"The day that man came in and attacked me in the bathroom… We couldn't figure out how anyone even knew I was with you. We figured if anyone from our trusted circle told, it was an accident. Or maybe someone from the hospital saw us leaving together or someone saw us in the car. But there *was* one person I know for sure who saw us together that day."

She looked over her shoulder in the direction of the elevators.

"The reporter who was talking to me next to the vending machines," she clarified. "The one you told me not to talk to again because you didn't like him."

Adrenaline surged within her. Along with a feeling of stupidity.

"The first time I met him was the morning before

the explosion on the way to my car, then the next day here… He even called me an action hero. What if *he's* the third person?" Rose's eyes widened as she turned back to James. A more sobering worry hit her. "And if he is, then where did he just come from?"

Rose didn't wait for an answer. Instead, she threw open Damon's hospital room door.

The scene inside only confirmed her new theory.

"Oh my God, James, call for help!"

The missing Deputy Cameron was lying on the ground, blood pooling around him. The hospital bed next to him was empty. Rose, having learned her lesson over the last few attacks, did something she hadn't yet done around James.

She pulled out her service weapon.

Then she was running back down the hallway.

"Sheriff's deputy down in Room 214," she yelled out to the nurses' desk as they came up to it. Someone screamed at the sight of her gun but Rose yelled off the rest of her instructions. "Suspect just left. Shut the hospital down, now!"

Then Rose really kicked it into gear.

She slammed open the door to the stairs and hoped the elevators were as slow as usual.

James didn't complain and instead ran down the two flights of stairs ahead of her. He hit the exit for the first-floor door before Rose even saw it. Which meant when she made it out to see the front of the elevators, she was already late to the fight.

The reporter pulled a gun up just as James swung around to grab her waist.

Rose could have flinched, ducked, dropped her

weight and let James do the rest, but there was more than one reason that she wore the nickname Wildcard so well.

She actually had some skill to back it up.

James put his arm around her and pulled her along with him to the corner of the hallway. Rose let it happen but she didn't turn around. Instead, she had her gun up and aimed.

Rose might have been known for running into danger without a plan but people often left out the part where, once she was in a situation, she didn't back down. If her boots made any noise as they slid across the floor, she didn't hear it.

The gunshot she let off was just too loud.

The reporter bellowed out in pain as her hit landed. The force and surprise must have offset his trigger finger to fire late. James was able to pull her the rest of the way around the corner before he could get a shot off.

The glass windows over the side parking lot exit shattered in response to the miss. Screams sounded in the distance. Someone cut in on the overhead announcement system, but Rose wasn't paying attention to anything else.

She stepped out of James's hold and yelled out to the reporter.

"Sheriff's department, throw your weapon away or—"

He apparently wasn't having it.

James cut her off.

"Listen! He's running!"

Rose quieted in time to hear a heavy bang. It wasn't a gunshot this time.

"He ran back into the stairwell!"

Rose led the charge to the door they had just come from and kicked it open. No shots or attack came their way.

There was blood, however. A trail ran up the stairs, dotting the concrete and giving them the direction they needed.

Rose peeked out between the floors and looked up. There was a small space between the railings. She could see all the way to the top floor.

The reporter wasn't waiting to catch sight of her and shoot. He was climbing up without stopping.

Rose didn't have a clear shot of him.

Which meant they chase was still on.

"Be careful," James ground out, but Rose was already running.

THE RAIN HAD slacked off, but the roof was still freshly wet.

Rose burst out from the stairwell and nearly fell because of it.

James was at her elbow and caught her quickly by the back of her shirt. Like in the hallway downstairs, the change in gravity didn't stop her. The instant her momentum swung back, she was on the man's heels, yelling again for him to drop his weapon.

This time he didn't turn and shoot. He also didn't stop.

The roof that they were on was one of three different heights along the hospital's main building. Right now they were on the middle height. It led to another roof that was a floor lower.

For a second, James thought the man would jump off their roof for the one below. It wouldn't be a fatal fall but there was no way it wouldn't hurt. It would also be hard for them to reach him without finding a ladder or going back inside to get to the stairwell that serviced the middle building.

He could try the escape, but it would cost him. And judging by the drops of blood they had been passing on the way there, he was already paying the price from Rose's earlier hit.

The man must have run the risk himself. He stopped near the edge of the roof.

Rose yelled out again for him to drop his weapon.

He didn't, but he did lower it to his side.

"Be careful," James urged again.

Rose kept her aim on the man and stalked forward, slowly walking at an angle as she went, as if making a half circle behind him. If he turned around to shoot, he would waste time adjusting his aim because of it. James followed her, trying to stay as quiet as possible while also staying close enough to Rose in case he needed to act.

Rose continued to watch the man. James eyed his gun.

"You're hurt," Rose said, voice carrying with authority across the shrinking distance. "Put the gun down and we can take you back inside for medical treatment."

The man barked out a laugh.

His words carried with just as much ease.

"You know, I called him an idiot."

James and Rose had made an arc around the man so now they stopped at the edge of the roof as well, just with several feet between them. The man stayed facing the edge, his profile showed his gun at his side and blood dripping down the same arm. Even though he had laughed, there was no smile there now.

"Who?" Rose asked.

"Damon Tillman. The man who was supposed to kill you but apparently didn't." The man laughed again. "I understood why he wanted to kill you, even if I thought it was a waste of time, but the way he *wanted* to kill you? Making a fool of *you* by showing everyone that the little action star could die as fantastically as the way you saved everyone else. I *laughed* at him for that. I really did. It was such a waste of time, such a waste of resources and money. And yet…" He sighed. "Now I wouldn't mind something grand to take you out too."

James balled his fist.

He didn't move, though.

He was acutely aware of Rose's body language.

James hadn't lied to her the night before. He didn't want her to stop being Wildcard Rose. He didn't need that from her or for her. She was who she was.

James didn't need her to give up anything to make space for him.

He was already at her side, ready.

And he wanted it to always be like that.

Especially in the tough spots.

So James stayed his steps and waited for her move. The second she did was the second before he did too.

"You're talking like you didn't have any part in the attacks against me," she called out. "I find that hard to believe."

The man didn't bother even looking their way.

"Why would I take revenge on you?" he asked. "Revenge costs money, patience. Emotional torment. It's a waste. I don't even get out of bed unless I'm getting paid to do it and you think I'm going to budget men with guns and car bombs?"

He shook his head.

"Love is nice but money? Money is life."

He lowered his head.

A breeze swept through. Rose's hair moved with it. The woman, however, was as still as a statue.

"Then why did you get involved with Damon and Lloyd and Camden Pharmaceuticals?" Rose tried. "If you thought what Damon was doing was ridiculous, why do you need to come here and deal with him at all?"

She was giving out details they hadn't yet confirmed.

And the man didn't hesitate to answer.

"Because I thought they understood that money is always the goal. That love doesn't pay the bills. It doesn't fix the broken air conditioner or pay for college. They understood how expensive the world is… But that didn't stop Damon from letting his love for his brother fester into guilt and anger. That didn't stop Lloyd from letting his love for his sister become some self-imposed sacrifice. And that didn't stop them from deciding to keep you alive when their death and yours would have kept me from killing Miss Harrison as a consequence."

He lifted his head again but still didn't look their way. He coughed before continuing. James saw blood come out. Rose had done more damage than James had thought.

"I don't understand any of you," he continued. "Damon spends a fortune trying to kill you, but in the end, he spares you. And now you're here, trying to get me, someone who never hated you, in some—what?—kind of sympathy for him? For Lloyd?"

Rose didn't answer. Instead she asked an important question, belatedly.

"Who are you?"

The man laughed one more time.

Rose shifted just a little at the noise.

"Someone who has a question."

Rose slid one foot back ever so slightly.

James realized she was shoring up her stance.

He waited, tense.

The man didn't wait for her reply.

He sighed out long. James could see blood from his mouth even in profile.

"Would you let me go if I offered you two money? More than you'll probably ever make in this lifetime? Would you walk away then?"

James watched as Rose moved her finger from next to the trigger to on top of it.

He reached out and placed a hand on her hip.

"No," she answered. "I won't let you get away with what you did to them. To Damon and Lloyd. To their family. Not for any price."

The man turned, gaze finally landing on hers.

He looked genuinely confused.

"Damon wants you dead and you're still trying to help him," he said. "Why?"

Rose answered him coolly. James realized later that she must have known already that it would be the last words she'd say to the man.

Her words were soft yet strong.

"Because it's what heroes do."

The man raised his gun, aiming right at them.
James didn't move a muscle.
Rose did.
The man never got a shot off.
Wildcard Rose had already pulled her trigger.

Chapter Twenty-One

Everyone thought Damon had fled the hospital, but to their utter surprise, he had only gone as far as the next room. Wynonna apologized profusely on his behalf.

"I saw that man in the lobby when I was downstairs," she told Rose, describing the reporter to a tee. "I recognized him. I never knew his name but he visited the house around the time Derrick passed away. Him and Lloyd got into a big yelling match. I never heard what they said but I remembered Damon left with him. It was actually the last time I saw Damon until now."

After seeing him, Wynonna had pieced together the same conclusion Rose had. Someone else had to have been pressuring her brother and Damon. She hadn't known all of the facts but that feeling, coupled with impressive speed, had gotten her to take Damon to the only safety she could reach. Deputy Cameron had come in during the brief moment between her coming in and the reporter showing up. He too had gotten a bad feeling from the man, and when Cameron had asked to see his hands, the reporter had attacked. Cameron hadn't been shot but knocked around good enough that he'd gotten a broken nose and a concussion.

Not too bad considering the man who had attacked him had died on the roof no more than ten minutes later.

That man remained nameless for one more week until finally Damon was able to talk.

And talk he did. To Rose first, of all people.

"His name was Paul Martinez. He hired me and Lloyd to copy and then disrupt the Camden Pharmaceuticals drug trial data. Paul was getting paid by Camden's competitors and was paying us a lot to help. We needed the money to clear some debt and, since the drug only treats insomnia, we decided it was the lesser of evils if we botched it instead of some of the other Camden drugs that help treat sicknesses." Damon had quieted. Rose had given him the space to get to the hard part of his confession. "The day of the storm, the generator didn't work, and the backup power cycled wrong. Instead of everything being shut down, they actually got some of the power back for the computers before they left on the bus. Lloyd said that's how Derrick saw the encrypted message he had been trying to send out before. It was highly incriminating for Lloyd. And me."

His eyes had grown red at that.

"Derrick was always smart, but I don't know why he chose to confront Lloyd on the bus. Not when it was already dangerous. Maybe…maybe he was really upset and afraid and it just came out. But no matter the reason why, he confronted Lloyd on the bus. And well, you were the only person who saw what happened next."

Damon had said that was when their faux reporter Paul had stepped in.

"Lloyd said that there was no way you heard what they were fighting about, but Paul was never one to let his money be in danger. He thought you might know something and when he saw how angry I was at you… he played on that anger to try and get you out of the way. Just like us, who had made too much trouble in his book. He wanted all three of us to go out at once. And what better way to have that happen without anyone looking too deep into it?"

"Your revenge against me," Rose had guessed.

Damon had nodded.

"When he realized I couldn't get you myself, he told us how to stage our deaths and, if we didn't listen, he threatened Wynonna."

Paul had given Damon and Lloyd proof that men were watching the young woman. Men they couldn't protect her from.

It had scared them enough to accept their final scene together.

The betrayal Damon had told Rose about referred to Paul's betrayal of them, not Lloyd's betrayal of him.

"No matter what we went through in this life, we never turned on each other," Damon had said, choking up a bit as he did so. "Lloyd was my person and Wynonna was *our* person. Even when we didn't agree with each other's decisions, we never lost sight of each other."

That was why they had accepted what they believed to be their only option left.

Their lives for Wynonna's.

But to Damon's surprise, when it came to killing Rose in the end, both men had decided, without even speaking, to give her a fighting chance.

Damon was good at tying knots but had left hers loose in case Lloyd had thrown her in. Lloyd had watched Damon go over the edge of the dock but had left Rose alone.

"I think Paul would have left you alone had we both died, especially if you didn't go after him or bring up anything about Camden. But you saved me."

Damon had looked at her then with an expression that she couldn't decipher.

Unlike Paul, he didn't ask her why.

Rose had been glad for that. She decided she was over talking about heroes.

Everyone involved had simply made choices.

Some hadn't worked out, some had.

MONTHS LATER AT Damon's trial, Rose would speak on his behalf for a lighter prison sentence. Wynonna would thank her after.

"I know it's not the same as Lloyd being there, but no matter what happens, I'm going to make sure Damon is never alone. Just like he did for me and my brother."

Rose didn't know Lloyd well, but she imagined he would have been proud of Wynonna's decision.

During all the trial and its aftermath, the drug trial at the research annex would be shut down for an extensive investigation that would reach into Camden Pharmaceuticals and its competitors, finding two more cases of attempted tampering with other trials elsewhere. Rose would keep up with the public updates but eventually would decide to stop after a while. Paul was gone, Damon and Wynonna were trying to heal, and Rose had finally shaken the press's fascination with her.

They had all done their parts and it was time to move on.

And move on they did.

Once the investigation closed, the insurance people finally got everything they needed for James and his father. Keller Auto was rebuilt and had a grand opening party that nearly the entire town of Seven Roads attended. The sheriff's department was the most vocal about their excitement. Mainly because, like Rose, most of the staff had fallen for the only mechanic in town.

James had been a sight and a half, standing next to the old service pit they had jumped into, with a smile on his face and a baby in his arms.

"And *this* is where Rose Little fell for me," he joked.

"Didn't you technically fall after *her*?" Price teased, his daughter Winnie punching him in the arm as a warning to behave himself. He kept on with a laugh. "You know, *after* she pulled you off a bomb?"

James waved his free hand through the air, careful to not jostle the newest member of the McCoy County Sheriff's Department family. Her father, the sheriff, was standing near them holding the hand of his other daughter while Blake held on to their son. They laughed along with Rose's parents as they had come in.

While they had wished Rose would have had a less dangerous experience while meeting a man she liked, they couldn't argue with the results. Her father had also taken a liking to Mr. Keller, both men prone to walking around the shop when they were in town and chatting about who-knew-what. Mr. Donahue, one of James's favorite people she realized quickly despite James pretending that he didn't like the man's constant chatting, was also there and more than ready to mingle.

And when Rose and James were married, he even cried.

But before all of that moving on happened, James

had taken Rose home from the hospital that night and then to bed.

They were tired, through and through, but somewhere and sometime between the sheets, James held her close and sighed out long.

"I have another good news, bad news thing but I think it might make me sound a little needy," he said, all soft and warm.

The lights were off but Rose still glanced up at him from her spot resting against his chest. She had already gotten used to this position, it making her fall asleep faster than anything else. But now she made sure to fight that urge.

"Bad news first this time," she decided. "I'd like to end today on a good note if we can."

She felt him nod.

"Bad news, I realized today that you didn't actually say if you liked me too," James said. "I mean I said it and then we had a great time and all after, but who knows, that might be Rose Little speak for I like you all right but not *that* much."

Rose struggled to keep a laugh in her chest and out of her next words.

"Ah, and the good news?"

"The good news is, even if you don't like me, I have all of this free time until the new shop is up and operating, so getting you to fall for me should be a piece of cake."

Rose lost it at that. She laughed against him until he was laughing with her too.

He started to stroke her back when they finished. Knowing him, that could have been the end of the conversation, at least that night.

But Rose decided to tease him because there was just something about James Keller that made her feel comfortable, safe, and loved enough to do so, even with such an important topic.

"How about I make you a deal?" she said. "You buy me some blackout curtains so I can sleep in on my off days, and I'll like, love, and stay with you for as long as you want?"

Rose's head bounced up and down a little as James let out a hoot of laughter.

"What?" she asked, worried the joke had been too much.

James kept going. Only after a moment did he get his words out.

"If that's all it takes, then I can't wait for you to see what's supposed to be delivered tomorrow."

Sure enough, the next day just after lunch a package came in.

It was the set of blackout curtains James had already bought two days prior.

A month later, Rose officially moved in. Five months after that they were married in the field behind the house.

James would go on to confuse everyone in attendance when he credited their entire love to a set of curtains.

Rose, however, would absolutely smile.

* * * * *